THE MARRIAGE BARGAIN

HEIDI KIMBALL

OTHER TITLES BY HEIDI KIMBALL

A Guarded Heart

An Unlikely Courtship

Maiden in the Tower

A Christmas Courting

Coming March 2020:

Where the Stars Meet the Sea

Other titles in the Regency House Party: Havencrest Series

Miss Marleigh's Pirate Lord

The Vexatious Widow

Charmed by His Lordship

The Captain's Lady

Cover design: Victorine Lieske

This book is a work of fiction. Names, characters, places, and incidents either are products of the author's imagination or are used fictitiously. Any resemblance to actual persons, living or dead, events, or locales is entirely coincidental.

Heidi Kimball
https://www.authorheidikimball.com
First Printing: August 2019

❀ Created with Vellum

CHAPTER 1

The carriage door shut with a dull-sounding thud, and instinctively, Emmeline braced herself for the verbal assault she knew was coming. Anna had burned a hole in Mama's favorite gown and Mama had been in a foul mood ever since. Fouler than usual. And now Emmeline was trapped inside a carriage with her. Alone. The ride to the Ramsbury's residence would be brief, yet still far too long.

"I hope you are satisfied, Emmeline. If your aim was to displease me, you have accomplished it perfectly. You have proven yourself utterly and completely worthless." Mama's sharp tone filled the carriage.

Emmeline sucked in a breath, trying not to show how the words pierced her.

"Three seasons I've given you. Was it too much to ask that you form a profitable match? Help our family step into the circles of high society? The size of your dowry should have ensured that, even if you aren't much to look at." The limited light only showed the harsh angles of Mama's face, though Emmeline could imagine the hard set of her mouth.

When Emmeline failed to respond, Mama continued her tirade.

"Months of effort, the fortune that went into your wardrobe. And yet somehow you are continually passed over even by men three times your age." That wasn't precisely true, though there was no need for Mama to know that. "And it's no wonder, with how cold you are. You are a spiteful creature and have brought me nothing but disappointment and misery."

"I'm sorry, Mama." The apology rose to her tongue out of habit.

"If you were truly sorry we wouldn't find ourselves attending the final ball of the season shamed by your failure to secure an attachment."

Tears threatened at the thought of the long night—no, the long *months*—ahead. Weeks without end where Emmeline's failures would be touted on a daily basis.

"I warned you on our journey to London. You are finished. I'll not waste another moment on an ungrateful daughter who uses me so despicably. There will not be another season."

At that, Emmeline's stomach clenched. She'd half hoped it was another of Mama's empty threats. She still held out hope for a love match. It was how she'd endured the endless parade of men that were, in fact, three times her age. Surely Papa wouldn't...her mouth opened to protest.

Mama shook her head, almost as if she could read Emmeline's thoughts. "Your father agrees with me."

Of course. Though he wasn't unkind to Emmeline, Papa was almost always occupied with business and he never went against Mama's wishes. The poison of despair spread through Emmeline's veins. Now it wouldn't be months, but years with no one but Mama and her caustic friends for companionship. For a moment Emmeline couldn't breathe. It felt as though a band had been wrapped around her chest, tightening with every breath she took.

"Do *not* give way to tears." Mama leaned forward but not a single curl of her regal black coiffure moved from its place. "You may be a disappointment, but don't make yourself pitiable as well."

The carriage wheels rolled to a stop and Emmeline blinked twice, quickly. She'd learned long ago that tears only made things worse for her. She attempted to conceal her emotions under a mask of indifference, but she was no actress. Her bottom lip trembled.

Emmeline swallowed, though her throat was so tight the effort proved unsatisfying.

A moment later the carriage door swung open and a footman assisted both ladies down. They were ushered up the stairs and into the enormous and congested ballroom, which already promised to be the greatest crush of the Season.

Mama caught sight of the voluptuous Mrs. Higgins. With a firm grip on Emmeline's elbow that left no doubt as to her displeasure, Mama propelled them both through the crowd. Emmeline's already-frayed nerves grew taut with the press of warm bodies around her, the smell of sweat and too much perfume. She shook her head, trying to keep her composure. She wouldn't last much longer.

"Mrs. Drake! Miss Drake! Can you believe the end of the Season is upon us?" Mrs. Higgins called before they'd even reached her. Mama released her grip on Emmeline's elbow and hurried forward. The crowd pressed between them, and Emmeline lost sight of her captor.

She was so grateful for the reprieve, she almost sighed aloud—a few minutes to collect herself, to reassemble the armor that would shield her from the worst of Mama's barbs. Somehow tonight she'd let down her guard, allowed Mama's words to sink their claws into her and draw blood. She peered through the wall of intermingling guests, searching for a path to the verandah. She worked her way across the room and pushed open the balcony door.

For the first time that night, Emmeline could breathe. She sank against one of the large pillars. She was tired, she realized. Tired of holding that armor in place.

A rainstorm earlier in the day had swept away the heat, and cool evening air rushed through her lungs, calming her. The slight tremble of her hands abated as relief flowed into her limbs. A moment of peace.

Until she realized she wasn't alone. A man paced along the terrace with a purposeful stride, headed in her direction. Emmeline stepped back, hoping the evening shadows of purple and gray would hide her.

Yet before he drew any closer, the man turned, his face catching the light. Viscount Anslowe. He paused for a moment and stared out at the gardens, though Emmeline had the distinct impression his attention was on something entirely different than the view in front of him. A moment later he resumed his path in the opposite direction.

She watched him from the darkness. Though they'd never been introduced, they had attended the same events enough times for Emmeline to have taken note of the man's attractive features. The way he could charm a group of ladies with his singular smile and easy banter. But more than that, there seemed to be a kindness about him, a gentleness of manner in the way he treated people.

If only Mama's scheming had included someone like Lord Anslowe instead of so many unattractive men who were old enough to be her grandfather, and usually quite handsy. Maybe then she wouldn't have so fervently avoided their offers of marriage.

Without warning, he turned on his heel and returned to the ballroom.

A blend of voices drew Emmeline's attention to the door through which the viscount had disappeared. It seemed her peace was to be short-lived. Several matrons, fans in hand, gathered in a tight circle. She was about to move from her hiding place when the conversation became discernible.

"Will he really declare himself this evening?"

"Everyone knows it for a fact." The woman who answered spoke with conviction, as if daring anyone to question her.

"But who? Who does he plan to offer for?" asked another.

The topic of their conversation roused Emmeline's curiosity before she remembered she shouldn't be eavesdropping.

"I don't think he particularly cares. Rumor has it Lord Anslowe has a list of prospects. Goodness knows there are plenty of women with a dowry to suit his needs."

"What are his needs?" A timid voice asked the very question Emmeline wished to know.

"Someone with enough money to save his estate, of course. His father's gambling debts left him barely solvent. All he wants is to be free to pursue his passion for politics."

Strange how a few gossipers could lay out a man's life in the course of a short conversation. Did Lord Anslowe *feel* trapped? She couldn't imagine it.

A scoff. "But why would he wait until the end of the Season when all of the prime fruit has already been picked?"

"He was too busy with his beloved Parliament to be bothered. And he knows he can snap his fingers and have any number of women who fit the bill."

"I suppose so."

Emmeline really should be getting back to Mama, though she dreaded it. She fiddled with her glove a moment.

"But *who* do you suppose?"

"Miss Jennings, with her twelve thousand. Mark my words."

"Why would he agree to put up with her constant wailing when he could have the pretty Miss Hastings for only a few thousand less?"

Did Lord Anslowe truly not care who he married? All at once, her heart began to pound erratically, as an idea took shape in her mind. Though such an arrangement would fall far short of a love match, at least she would be making her own choice.

She worried her lip and took a moment to think. What might she say to entice him?

No, it was too bold. Too daring. But she was desperate. Ready to try anything if it meant escaping Mama's plans for her. The worst he might say was no, leaving her in the precise position she found herself now—unattached and stuck with a mother unwilling to let her forget it. Stowed away into a bleak and miserable future of spinsterhood.

A strange weightless sensation overtook Emmeline at the thought of what she was considering. She slipped around the pillar and moved to the far door, reentering the ballroom.

She surveyed the crowd, looking for someone of Lord Anslowe's height. His chestnut brown hair that always looked a bit rumpled, as if he couldn't be bothered to do it properly. There. He hadn't made it very far into the ballroom. He stood in a small circle with Miss Hastings at his side.

She took the opportunity to study Miss Hastings. She was a far sight prettier than Emmeline, with her golden hair and sparkling blue eyes. But her teeth were crooked while Emmeline's were straight. She shook her head. What a silly thing to consider.

When she looked next Lord Anslowe was leading Miss Hastings and her ten thousand pounds away. To dance? To the verandah? Where he was planning to propose? It was now or never.

They were coming Emmeline's way. She stood only a few feet away from the door that led out to the balcony. Her stomach knotted up and her lungs seemed to have forgotten how to draw in air. Closer.

Lord Anslowe leaned toward Miss Hastings. "You have many enticing qualities, Miss Hastings."

Before she could stop herself, Emmeline reached out and laid a hand on Lord Anslowe's sleeve. He turned and suddenly the full weight of his gaze was upon her. "Pardon me, Lord Anslowe, but I must speak to you." Somehow, she forced strength and purpose into her voice. "It is a matter of some urgency."

His mouth twisted with a hint of curiosity. Somewhere in the back of her mind, Emmeline noted the perturbed expression that had crossed Miss Hastings face, but with Lord Anslowe's deep brown eyes upon her, she barely gave it thought.

Would he agree to speak with her? A woman he'd never been introduced to? She couldn't begin to guess what he might be thinking. He turned back to Miss Hastings. "You'll excuse me a moment, won't you?"

"Of course." Miss Hastings gave Emmeline a pinched look before releasing his arm.

Emmeline exhaled. Lord Anslowe fixed his attention upon her, as if waiting for her to do or say something. "Perhaps we could step outside?" she managed. Drat her breathy voice.

He nodded, still staring at her. She preferred enjoying his handsome features when his eyes weren't boring into her. "Shall we?" he said at last, extending his arm.

This time the cool air on the balcony was anything but calming. In fact, all alone with Lord Anslowe, it seemed rather warm. Her mouth was suddenly dry. When was the last time she'd spoken to anyone outside of Mama's hearing? With her pulse thrumming in her ears, Emmeline dove right in, afraid she would otherwise lose her nerve. "You'll excuse me for being so bold, Lord Anslowe. I heard you were in the market for a wife."

He cocked his head.

She went on, determined to get it all out before he could speak. "My source insisted you weren't overly particular about who, so long as the woman possesses a large dowry."

Lord Anslowe swallowed, seeming to overcome his surprise. "And who is your *source*, if I might inquire?"

Heat rose in her cheeks. How she wished for a fan. "Does it matter?"

A smile brushed the corners of his mouth. "I suppose not, though I'd be curious to know."

Perhaps easing into her proposal wouldn't hurt. "Very well. I overheard it from a circle of gossiping matrons."

Now there was real mirth in his eyes. "I see. Then I may as well confirm what they said is true. I *am* looking for a wife. And the size of her dowry *does* matter. I must be practical, after all."

"Yes, of course," she agreed. "That is precisely why I wished to speak to you. I am practical-minded as well."

He inclined his head. "An admirable quality." Something in the tone of his voice made her think him sincere.

"Yes, well." She was making a fool of herself and now her little speech had been completely overturned. "But to my point. I would like to propose an arrangement. A bargain, really. You need a wife with a dowry. I would like to offer myself as a willing candidate."

"Indeed?" he said, almost under his breath.

"I have a dowry of fifteen thousand pounds to recommend me."

The only indication of surprise came in the form of the smallest lift of his brow. Then he gave a nod, as if in approval. Emmeline's breath grew stilted. It seemed as though her lungs were trying to inhale and exhale simultaneously.

He leaned back against the pillar, crossing one leg over the other in a casual stance. "I suppose I am fortunate you intercepted me before I offered for Miss Hastings. Is that who the matrons predicted I would propose to?"

"Yes. Better her than the wailing Miss Jennings."

He flashed a grin. "Of course. But you have a dowry of 15,000 pounds. Why were you overlooked as a possibility?"

Emmeline tried not to flinch at his question. Better to be upfront about the matter. "My father's money comes from trade, my lord."

He did the last thing she expected. He laughed. "You should know there's nothing I like better than upending the old gossips' expectations, so that counts as a point in your favor. What, exactly, are you hoping to get out of this arrangement? You don't seem the type to fawn over titles, which is all I can really claim as an enticement."

Emmeline rubbed her elbow, still sore from Mama's bruising grip. "I am looking to escape my mother, Lord Anslowe."

"A veritable she-dragon is she?"

She gave a little shrug, trying not to show how much depended on this conversation. How her entire future seemed to hang in the balance. "You might say that."

His mouth pressed into a firm line. Indicating what, Emmeline couldn't say. "So if I understand you correctly, if I ask you to be my wife you will agree?"

She hesitated. "Well, I think it might be wise for us to come to some sort of agreement about exactly what this arrangement would entail."

"Besides marriage?"

"Within marriage."

"It sounds like you have some specifics in mind. Please go on."

She took a moment to collect her thoughts. There was no sense in rushing through this now that she had his attention. "I know politics are important to you," she said finally.

One brow went up, and she could practically feel the waves of amusement rolling off him. But she went on doggedly. "You would stay here, in London. I have always wanted my own household. I could live in the country and oversee the matters of your estate." It was perfect, really. "We would correspond, of course. To exchange any necessary information. And you could come for visits every other month, stay for a day or two while you see that everything meets your satisfaction."

The whole thing sounded preposterous. Her breath hitched as she awaited his reply.

"And what about an heir?"

She hadn't expected that, though of course she should have. To speak of such matters to a relative stranger! A fierce blush burned every inch of her skin. "The pressing reason for you to marry is the dowry, not an heir. That could come...later."

"In an arrangement like this, I think it is best to be specific." An indolent smirk. "How much later? One year? Two?"

"Five," she managed, proud that her voice didn't break. "I mean, since you'll be in London and I'll be..."

"You are practical, as you said." He was fully grinning now. "Anything else?"

"I think that is all." Her mouth grew dry under his scrutiny.

"So we have a bargain?"

She could only nod.

He stepped toward her, and Emmeline suddenly questioned the wisdom of proposing such an arrangement with someone so handsome. She needed to keep a clear head. The man was only marrying her for her money. And she was only marrying him to escape Mama's clutches. Thank goodness the parameters they'd set would help her remember that.

"Well then, if I may?" His warm brown eyes took on a little glint.

She nodded her assent.

He stepped forward and took her hand in his. She could scarcely breathe. Never in her life did Emmeline expect for a man to look at her the way Lord Anslowe was looking at her now. His gaze was heavy, riveting.

"Will you marry me?" He spoke low, and the rich timbre of his voice sent a shiver down Emmeline's spine.

"Yes. I will." Breathe, she reminded herself.

He leaned closer. "One more question, if I may be so bold?"

Emmeline nodded again, trying to project a calm she didn't feel.

"Would you be so good as to tell me your name?"

CHAPTER 2

LONDON: ONE YEAR LATER

*A*nslowe whistled as he picked up his riding gloves from the bedside table. He couldn't remember the last time he'd had a free afternoon. Today the skies were clear save for a few wispy white clouds that didn't hold enough rain to soak a handkerchief. He brushed at his riding pants, anxious to be astride his horse.

With Parliament adjourned for the summer, he could finally take the time for some more leisurely pursuits. Not that he wasn't already planning for the next session. There were alliances to be made, votes to pursue. He really should arrange for a meeting with Lord Sotheby, but since the man was summering in Brighton, that could come later.

At the bottom of the stairs, Anslowe found Barnett waiting for him with a tray of letters. "Anything interesting?" He knew the man couldn't help but nose through his correspondence.

His stately butler gave an affronted sigh. "I'm sure I wouldn't know, my lord."

Anslowe shot him a knowing look.

Barnett cleared his throat. "A letter from Lady Anslowe. And, well, there is something from Mrs. Garvey," he amended.

His aunt? He hadn't heard from her for several months. He sorted through the letters on the tray until he found the one that bore her handwriting. His ride could wait a moment. His aunt and her grievances never failed to entertain.

He opened the letter and began to read. But today the contents of her letter did not amuse him. His gut tightened the further he read. When he finished he thrust his gloves into Barnett's waiting hands and turned on his heel, straight toward his study. He penned hasty messages to his friends, asking them to meet him at White's.

He arrived at the club well before his friends. He sat back in the deep-set leather chair and pulled out Emmeline's letter.

The overabundance of rain has led to some flooding, and many of the surrounding estates have sustained losses, but Mr. Smith's foresight, once again, proved almost prophetic. He has handled everything perfectly. I am sure, come your visit at the end of this month, you will find everything to your satisfaction...

Anslowe rubbed his neck as he examined the flawless script. He had read the letter three times, searching for *something* that might indicate his wife was addressing her husband, rather than a passing acquaintance. The bottom was simply signed, *Yours, Etc., Lady Anslowe.* Well, she bore his name at least.

He set the letter down on the table, thinking over the past year. Per their arrangement, he saw Emmeline every two months. Yet he hardly knew her. For each of their visits she was polite but stiff. She had an air of guardedness that made anything but talk of the estate or their finances difficult. He'd always attributed it to natural reserve, but perhaps he'd been wrong. Perhaps it was all an act.

He'd been waiting at his table for almost an hour when footsteps sounded behind him. Buxton hefted himself into the chair to Anslowe's right, puffing out a breath of air that pushed his hair up in a flutter. Dunkirk followed, easing into the chair across from him with a bit more decorum. He inclined his head toward the letter resting in Anslowe's hand. "Bad news?"

"I'm not certain."

Dunkirk inclined his head, taking the liberty of reading some of the letter. "Are you worried about the flooding? It sounds like your steward has everything well in hand."

Anslowe shook his head. "No, not that." He lowered his voice. "It's my marriage."

It was almost comical how both men leaned forward in unison.

Buxton spoke first. "Oh ho! Trouble in paradise? How is such a thing possible? You have the perfect arrangement. A wife you rarely have to see and never have to attend to."

"It's not that." Anslowe patted his coat, where he'd stowed the other letter. "I've received a letter from my aunt. She informed me there are rumors circulating. Rumors that Emmeline has...well, that she's been unfaithful." His stomach felt as though it were full of lead. "Have you heard anything to that effect?"

Dunkirk shrugged. "I've been asked, but there are always rumors flying about. No one gives them much credence."

"They will when the rumor involves my wife and my greatest political foe."

Buxton gaped. "Lord Wembley."

"The very man."

"Surely this ill-conceived rumor will fade into obscurity," interjected Dunkirk. "It cannot be true."

Anslowe's cheek muscle twitched. "My aunt lives in Brighton. If the rumors have reached her ears, they will not die easily."

"Would Lady Anslowe have taken on a lover?" Buxton was direct as always.

"Of course not." Though he didn't feel nearly as confident as he sounded. It struck him then, how very little he knew of his own wife. "The timing is terrible. I'd hoped to spend the summer traveling and garnering support for my bill. But I can't possibly do that while my wife is living under a cloud of speculation." As common as philandering was among married couples in society, the thought made him rather ill.

Dunkirk adjusted his cravat. "What can you do?"

Anslowe rubbed at his jawline, late afternoon stubble scraping against the back of knuckles. "My aunt has suggested I bring Emmeline to her house party. There will be an assortment of wealthy and titled guests. It would be a good place to see and be seen. We could lay the rumors to rest. And my uncle is good friends with Prinny. Such a connection could be pivotal. Lord Sotheby will also be there." He grinned.

"It seems like you've got it all figured out."

"Not quite. I have to get Emmeline to agree. I can't just snap my fingers and expect her to do my bidding."

"Why ever not?" Buxton signaled to one of the waiters to bring him a drink.

"Because we have our bargain. And if I don't uphold my end of the bargain, she might not be inclined to hold up hers." Understanding dawned on both of their faces. They knew the arrangement that had been agreed to by Emmeline and himself, or at least the basic gist of it.

What he had never explained was that the whole idea of marriage had been Emmeline's idea. He knew exposing that truth would mortify her, and for a reason he couldn't explain, Anslowe wanted to protect her from it. To shield her from the embarrassment it would surely cause her.

Though perhaps he wouldn't feel quite so chivalrous if the rumors turned out to be true.

All of them mulled over the problem silently.

Dunkirk nodded. "He's got a point. You should never give a woman the upper hand. They always use it against you. There must be a way to go about this without upending the bargain you were fortunate enough to negotiate."

"Why can't you just use your charm? Women are always more than willing to give you whatever you want." A hint of envy lined Buxton's tone.

Anslowe shook his head and set down the letter. "Emmeline isn't the kind that can be charmed. I need..." He blew out a breath. "I need something. Something to negotiate with."

"Now there's an idea. You need something she wants. In order to get it, she has to join you at the house party."

Anslowe stared at his hands. "The question is, what does she want?"

* * *

EMMELINE DREW IN A DEEP BREATH, admiring the ripples in the pond. The sun beat down without reservation, not a cloud in the sky. She'd walked farther than usual this morning and sweat trickled down her back. June had been full of rain, but the first part of July had been unseasonably hot.

It was only ten minutes back to the house, but the distance felt daunting. Normally Emmeline's morning walk energized her, but she hadn't slept well last night, and in the sweltering summer air she felt well and truly exhausted.

The large pond looked more inviting than ever, the sun glinting off its calm surface. A quick survey of the area assured Emmeline she was alone. Another rivulet of sweat worked its way down her chemise, past the line of her stays. That decided it. She removed her bonnet, half boots and stockings. For a moment she considered removing her dress, but there was always the chance that the groundskeeper or one of his crew might pass through.

Though she'd been her own mistress for nearly a year, she still felt guilt clench her insides whenever she did something which she knew her mother would disapprove of. But Mama wasn't here to voice her censure. Besides, there were things Mama did of which Emmeline disapproved—like encourage her father to become involved in the risky business of speculation.

With that in mind, she pushed back her shoulders, filled her lungs with air, and clasped her hands straight up over her head as she dove into the pond. The cool water enveloped her, slicing through her dress in half a second, soothing the sting of the sun. She surfaced, her chilled skin welcoming the warmth of the sun's rays.

She tilted back her head, floating on her back for a moment. Small ripples lapped at her cheeks, but the water muffled all other sound. Some of her hair had come loose from its pins and flowed around her head. She enjoyed the weightless feeling for a few minutes, the freedom of giving into a pleasure Mama never would have allowed her.

Had it only been a year since she'd approached Lord Anslowe and offered herself as a candidate to be his wife? For her, the time had flown by. Though with every visit her husband made she became more and more determined to keep her distance. It would be far too easy to fall prey to his charms.

He had more than any man ought.

The frigid water began to numb her limbs, and Emmeline tilted her head up and began to work toward a shallower bank. It took longer than it should have with her dratted dress weighing her down. Every time she kicked, her feet caught in the folds of her dress. It was not enough to make swimming impossible, just awkward.

She reached the bank and climbed out of the water. After spending a few minutes wringing out her dress and smoothing back her hair, she gathered her things and headed back toward Chelten House. Sometimes as she approached its lovely white façade with its ongoing rows of windows after her morning walks, she still couldn't believe she was mistress of such a place.

Emmeline slipped through the back door. She was still quite wet and wished it wasn't necessary to go through the front entry, dripping water all over the marble floors, in order to reach the staircase.

She reached the main entry and set foot on the stairs.

"Emmeline?"

She froze. Her pulse drummed through her veins. The baritone voice she recognized, yet her mind couldn't quite make sense of it. The owner of that voice was supposed to be in London for another two weeks. It was what they'd agreed upon. Lord Anslowe had never, in a full year of marriage, shown up unexpectedly.

She turned, cursing herself for giving into the impulse for a morning swim.

Lord Anslowe stood in the middle of the entry, as if he'd only just arrived. His hair was a little unkempt, a cavalier smile on his face.

Emmeline suppressed a groan. She must look a sight. The way

Lord Anslowe's eyes roamed over her, mouth slightly ajar, confirmed it. She cleared her throat and forced a smile. "Lord Anslowe." She curtsied, her dress still clinging to her legs, water pooling on the stairs. "How very good of you to…" There wasn't quite a word for it. She couldn't label him a visitor in his own home. "Drop in," she finished.

This wasn't part of the bargain.

CHAPTER 3

*E*mmeline gave a brief curtsy. "If you will excuse me, I need to go and change out of these wet things."

Anslowe stared at his wife's retreating figure as she made her way up the stairs. His chest felt as though it had been struck by an anvil. There wasn't any other way to describe the shock of seeing his wife's figure perfectly outlined by her soaking dress. Her hair disheveled and flowing about her shoulders. She looked so very different from the prim and proper woman he'd grown accustomed to meeting. So very…womanly.

Over the last year, he'd grown to respect Emmeline's mind, her quick thinking, and the ease with which she handled all of the matters of the estate. His visits every two months were more a formality than a necessity, as she always had everything well in hand. The bargain they'd agreed to had made them partners whose discussions centered around the affairs of the estate. But somewhere during those visits he'd lost sight of what an attractive woman he'd married.

More than anything, he was taken aback by the wave of jealousy that swept through him when he thought of the rumors his aunt alluded to in her letter. He revolted at the very thought of Emmeline with another man. Be it his political rival, his steward, or one of the footmen. He'd never felt so protective of anyone or anything, and certainly not a woman who was his wife in nothing but name.

He rubbed at his jaw and tried to gather his bearings. He needed his wits about him if he was going to get Emmeline to agree to attend the house party with him.

The sound of surprise made by Mrs. Hanover, the housekeeper, startled him from his thoughts. "My lord," she said, curtsying. "Shall I call for some refreshments to be brought?"

"Yes," he said, hardly giving the matter thought.

"In the blue salon?" she asked.

He nodded. "Inform Lady Anslowe I shall wait for her there." He strode away, trying to reform his plan given this surprising turn in events.

One thing became clear. No longer was he content with the status quo. He was done being nothing more than a business partner who discussed the needs of the tenants and the latest renovations on the estate. Whether Emmeline knew it or not, this charade of a marriage was about to change—he was done with their ridiculous bargain.

She might believe he'd married her only for her dowry, but the truth was, he'd been captivated by her boldness, by the forthright manner in which she'd approached him. He'd been surprised and delighted by her proposition, even a little thrown off balance.

Now it was his turn to set her world askew. Charm. He needed to muster every ounce of charm he possessed if he hoped to convince Emmeline to attend the house party with him.

The woman who occupied his thoughts appeared in the doorway a quarter of an hour later. She had changed from the dark and sodden dress into a flattering dress with white and navy blue pinstripes, but the flowing fabric of the gown did little to distract him from the curves they hid. He stood at once and forced his eyes upward.

She braced herself, posture tensing. Her lips drew together, forming a disapproving line. "What's happened? What is wrong?"

The space between his brows pinched. "Wrong? Nothing is wrong."

Her voice sounded almost accusatory. "You weren't due home for another two weeks."

"Now, now." He gave her his trademark grin that made people believe he hadn't a care in the world. "You mustn't show too much enthusiasm when greeting your husband."

A flush climbed up her neck and straight onto her cheeks. Before she had a chance to regain her composure, he chose a topic he knew would fluster her. "So, tell me. Did you trip and fall into one of the fountains?"

She blew out a breath and clasped her hands firmly together. "No, I...I was out walking, and the heat was unbearable. I cooled myself off in the pond."

He raised a brow. Surprising. That hadn't been what he'd expected at all.

"Lord Anslowe, to what do I owe the pleasure?"

Anslowe neatly sidestepped her question. "Emmeline, you're looking well." His eyes grazed over her appreciatively, though he rather preferred the soaking gown that had highlighted her figure. Brighton's beaches were quite popular; perhaps he could talk her into taking a dip in the sea.

"Thank you." She was about to take a seat, but he reached for her hand and brushed a kiss over her knuckles. Her hand froze under his touch. She cleared her throat and he released her, pleased to note how the simple gesture affected her. Would a woman carrying on behind his back be brought to blush so easily? It didn't seem likely. Though perhaps she was a much better actress than he gave her credit for.

Anslowe stepped back, waiting until she'd taken a seat before he took his own. "I know my arrival is unexpected." He pulled something from his jacket pocket. "I received an invitation, or perhaps *summons* would be a more appropriate term, from my aunt."

"A summons?" she echoed.

"My aunt and uncle live in Brighton. Much to my aunt's chagrin, my uncle always hosts a rather lavish house party over the summer. She is all but demanding our presence."

She stiffened, almost imperceptibly. Almost. "You should go, of course. You mustn't disappoint your aunt."

He shook his head. "I couldn't go alone. Besides, I have been meaning to introduce you to my aunt and uncle for some time. The Garveys. I'm sure I have mentioned them."

"But the renovations on the guest wing have only just commenced. Right now is not—"

He had done his research and knew which cards to play, should it prove necessary. But for now, he tried with simple persuasion. "It is only for ten days. Surely you can be spared that long. A man likes to show off his wife now and again."

She raised her eyes to his, the color of rich coffee. "I am needed here."

"Not as much as I need you to accompany me."

Tension crackled between them.

"Our bargain never included visits to one another's families." Insistence colored her tone.

"If you accompany me to my aunt's house party, I'll willingly visit your parents if you wish it." He challenged her with his gaze.

"No!" she said fervently. "No. I have no interest in you accompanying me to visit my parents."

"No? Perhaps not. But I think you'd very much like to travel abroad, to see the Continent. Paris, Berlin, Venice, Rome. Any three cities of your choosing. We could go in September, right as the weather begins to cool."

The look on her face told Anslowe he'd gained the upper hand. Much as she tried to rein in her eagerness, it was etched in the brightness of her eyes, the anxious lines around her mouth.

"What do you think, Emmeline? A ten-day house party in exchange for several months abroad?" Though he knew her answer, he waited for her to voice it.

Emmeline straightened her back and smoothed her skirts. "I'll inform Bridget to begin packing at once. When do we leave?"

Only a hard-won battle against his natural impulse kept a self-satisfied grin from turning up the corners of his mouth.

CHAPTER 4

Though the carriage ride had been uneventful, the torrent of thoughts assaulting Emmeline had been anything but. Lord Anslowe had struck up some conversation, yet a good portion of the four-hour journey had passed in silence. In the quiet moments as they jutted along over the road leading to Brighton, she could feel her husband's eyes upon her: questioning, probing. His scrutiny caused a knot to form within her chest.

Emmeline could sense that something simmered beneath the surface of his casually positioned frame. There was certainly something more than a familial visit to his aunt that had motivated his desire to attend this house party, if only she knew what. He'd closed his eyes a few minutes before, so she seized the opportunity to take his measure without being found out.

Unlike her, who'd grown wrinkled and frumpy under the incessant bumping of the carriage, Lord Anslowe appeared unperturbed. His light brown hair fell in a careless wave across his forehead. His angled jaw held no tension, though his chin dipped down occasionally as the carriage jostled. That such a handsome man could be her husband was still difficult for Emmeline to fathom. Perhaps that was why she'd so recklessly agreed to his proposition yesterday. Nothing else could explain it.

Yesterday morning she'd been planning on picking out the final color scheme for the guest rooms and today she sat across from her husband, on her way to some lavish house party where she'd be forced into the uncomfortable company of gossipmongers and social climbers.

She'd been determined to refuse Lord Anslowe's pleas, and might have succeeded, had he not offered the one thing she'd always longed for: travel. How could he possibly have known how badly she ached to see the quaint streets of Paris, the ancient sites of Italy, the castles of Germany? But even under the allure of the promise of faraway cities, Emmeline feared for her heart. She knew the danger of spending too much time with her husband. Even with their limited interactions, the array of flutters that assaulted her midsection every time he glanced at her, testified of her foolishness.

The man was a polished politician, whose charisma made him welcome in every circle in London. She was the daughter of a tradesman, who at best felt uncomfortable among the upper echelons of society. Indeed, the only reason Emmeline had caught Lord Anslowe's attention was fortuitous timing and a sizeable dowry. It was irrational to even contemplate there being anything but spousal obligation between them. He hadn't even batted an eye when she'd put off the matter of an heir.

Lord Anslowe's eyes opened and he caught her staring. She blushed fiercely, grateful he couldn't read her thoughts.

"We're almost there," he said. "Have you looked out the window?"

She scooted toward the window so she could get a glimpse of Brighton. Her eyes widened as she took in the sweeping hills and the shimmering water. "Oh!" For the first time since she'd agreed to accompany her husband, she thought there might be a part of this trip she'd enjoy.

"You've never been to Brighton, I take it?"

"I have traveled very little. Mama always thought it was a—" She shook her head, cutting off the thought. "Liverpool has beaches, but they certainly don't look like this." She glanced back at her husband. "You're probably thinking it would be silly to take me abroad when I haven't even seen most of England."

"Not at all." He smiled. "It is better to travel abroad before we start our family."

Our family. She closed her eyes, willing away the blush rising on her cheeks. Time for a change in subject. "Do you have a favorite part of England?"

"Cornwall," he returned easily. "There's a wildness to the beaches there. And it isn't fashionable like Brighton. It truly feels like an escape."

"And what do you need to escape from?"

He shrugged. "Pressure, politics."

"I thought you loved politics."

"I did. I do. But sometimes…sometimes it doesn't bring me the fulfillment it used to." He gave a half smile, but it wasn't the charming version he used in ballrooms and assemblies, it was a genuine one, with just a hint of sadness behind it. "I suppose that means I'm growing old."

"You're only thirty-one."

"And you are twenty-two?"

She gave him a brief smile. "Next week."

His brow wrinkled so she clarified. "I turn twenty-two next week."

"Well, we will have to find some way to celebrate." The way he said *we* filled her with warmth.

She nodded, still preoccupied with the thought of having this man—her husband—here by her side for the next ten days. If this was what it would feel like she could grow accustomed to it very quickly. Suddenly their bargain and the separate lives she'd forced them to live felt much less like a wall that kept her safe and much more like a wall that kept her out. Perhaps she'd been wrong to insist so adamantly on the hollow nature of their relationship.

"Here we are," announced her husband. "Havencrest. Prepare yourself for my aunt's ridiculousness."

"And what of your uncle?"

24

"He is ridiculous in his own way. The two are constantly at odds."

A small yearning rose in her, to learn about her husband, to understand him. What did she know of him, really? His aunt and uncle perhaps had an unhappy marriage, but what of his parents? She knew they had both been killed in a carriage accident when he was nineteen, but had it been a marriage of tolerance? A love match? Did he hope for such within their own marriage?

She swatted away the idea like a pesky fly. To entertain any thought of a romantic relationship between them was pure madness. The man dished out compliments as if they were as plentiful as cotton. He had more women in love with him than he owned cravats. Only a fool would give her heart to such a man. Even if he was her husband.

The carriage rolled to a stop and the door swung open. A smartly dressed footman extended his hand and Emmeline took it, stepping down as she tried to gather her bearings. To label the house impressive was an aberrant understatement. And set against the splendor of Brighton's cliffs, the house and its grounds created a breathtaking view. A friendly breeze that smelled of salt and seaweed wafted by.

Several other carriages deposited guests, and Emmeline's stomach tightened, watching the display of wealth and finery that paraded up the stairs. She'd promised herself, once she left London behind, that she was finished with these types of events. Yet here she stood, once again, entirely out of her element.

Only this time it wasn't her disapproving mother who accompanied her. Lord Anslowe came and stood by her side. He held out his arm and motioned at the stairs leading up to the house. "Shall we?"

CHAPTER 5

*A*nslowe felt the trembling of Emmeline's hand as she slipped her arm into his. So unexpected, given how poised and self-assured she seemed at home. Yet her outward manner revealed not a hint of the unease he could sense within her.

They ascended the stairs where his aunt and uncle stood welcoming people in the entry hall. Aunt Garvey stood, her back straight, her thin frame attired in a dress that would have been fashionable two decades ago. Uncle Garvey stood at her side, his jovial demeanor the opposite of his wife in every way. Where she was thin, he was round. Her stern features were only emphasized by the smile lighting his face and the perpetual merriment in his eyes.

"I hope you didn't stop to change your horses," Aunt Garvey said by way of greeting. "Such an excess is rarely warranted."

"Ah, we meet your bride at last!" said his uncle, ignoring his wife's comment.

"This is my wife, Lady Anslowe," he said. She curtsied as he bowed. "And Emmeline, may I introduce my uncle and aunt, Mr. and Mrs. Garvey."

"Thank you for so generously inviting us to your house party."

Emmeline smiled, though her voice was hushed. "It is a pleasure to meet you both."

Aunt Garvey's eyes prowled over Emmeline, as if she might be able to ferret out the truth of the rumors she'd heard just by looking at her. "I've heard you are making repairs to Chelten House. I hope that is keeping you occupied."

Emmeline nodded. "Well, yes. I also—"

Aunt Garvey cut her off. "I think it is wise for a woman to keep herself occupied so she isn't tempted to become otherwise…engaged."

Anslowe only just suppressed a groan. The last thing he needed was for his aunt to ask Emmeline outright about rumors of the affair. Emmeline turned questioning eyes on him, but Uncle Garvey saved them both from answering.

"She's a shy little thing, isn't she?" He set a hand in his pocket. "But what a pretty smile. You'll warm up to us in no time. We've got a good deal of fun planned, I assure you. And Mrs. Daw will show you to your rooms."

Aunt Garvey gestured for them to go ahead. "Tea is being served in the drawing room if you need something to tide you over."

Anslowe knew the tea would be watery and the fare nonexistent. He shook his head. "I believe we are more in need of rest than nourishment. Come Emmeline. Perhaps you can lie down for a while before dinner." Her sigh of relief clearly expressed her feelings on the matter.

"I won't be joining you tonight," boomed his uncle, "as I've been summoned to join Prinny this evening. Accept my apologies in advance."

Anslowe immediately wondered if he might be fortunate enough to gain Prinny's ear long enough to make a case for his bill. "Of course."

Aunt Garvey crooked a pointed finger at the two of them. "Dinner is at seven. Don't be late. You know how I feel about people who aren't punctual."

"I am well aware, Aunt Garvey." He fought back the smile at his aunt's determined sharpness and guided Emmeline toward the waiting housekeeper, who welcomed them energetically.

"My lord, what a delight. I haven't seen you in an age! And now here you are, married, I see. It is a pleasure to have you and Lady Anslowe here at Havencrest."

"I thank you, Mrs. Daw. Lady Anslowe has endured a long day of travel and I hope to get her settled so she might rest before dinner."

"Yes, yes, of course. Follow me." She guided them up the stairs and to the left, down one of the spacious guest wings. They passed several other guests, but Anslowe focused his attention on Emmeline. He hoped she hadn't been too put off by Aunt Garvey.

"It's a beautiful home," Emmeline leaned toward him, whispering.

"Yes, and they have several others. Though this is my favorite. The windows make the place feel light and airy. The views are spectacular."

"Here we are," proclaimed Mrs. Daw in a sing-song tone. She pushed open the door, revealing a small but pleasant sitting room with a good-sized window that made it feel bigger than it was. "The party is so large not all the married couples were given separate rooms, but I believe Mrs. Garvey rather enjoyed ensuring her personal guests have the best accommodations."

Relief flooded Anslowe. It was enough that Emmeline had agreed to attend the house party with him—he wasn't sure how she would feel about being forced to share a bed during their stay.

"And just here I have some candles for you." Mrs. Daw set two used candles on the table, neither more than the length of his forefinger. "I wish I could offer you more, but I gave you the best we have. You know Mrs. Garvey—she prides herself on being, er, rather economical, if you recall."

"It hasn't been *that* long since I've visited, Mrs. Daw," he teased. "Never you fear. I had my valet pack enough extra candles, tea, and soap for the both of us."

The woman touched a hand to her heart. "Thank goodness. I fear everyone else will be making numerous trips into town." She turned to Emmeline who was studying the candles with a perplexed expression on her face. "Well, my lady. It is a pleasure. I hope you will not hesitate to ring if there is anything at all you need."

Emmeline removed her bonnet, laying it on a small table adjacent to the sofa. "Of course. Thank you for all of your help, Mrs. Daw."

The woman gave her a rosy-faced grin. "Of course, my lady." Mrs. Daw turned away, her stout figure disappearing through the door. She shut it quietly behind her.

Silence blanketed in the room, the only sound the soft swish of Emmeline's skirts as she approached the window. The silence was uncomfortable, filled with a strain that came from being in a shared space as husband and wife, when they had never truly lived that way.

Anslowe had never been one for silence, in society or in Parliament. He certainly wouldn't be so in marriage. "Emmeline," he began, then paused a moment.

She half turned, as if to show him she was listening.

"Thank you for being here with me." He'd not given a great deal of thought as to what it would be like to have his wife on his arm as he navigated society, but he found he rather liked it.

Emmeline raised her head, pulling him from his musings. "It is nothing more than any wife would do, my lord."

"Perhaps not one who detests society as much as you seem to."

She fully turned then, eyes wide with surprise. "I'm sorry it is so evident."

"It isn't. But why do you hate it so much?"

She fingered the small locket at her throat, her deep brown eyes searching him. "I…I had three seasons. All were painful. I believe most young girls think of it as a time of excitement. Balls and dresses and the attention of fawning gentlemen."

He nodded slightly to acknowledge her point.

"For me every ball was an endless round of lecturing from Mama about how to act, what to say, how everything I did was wrong. She criticized my dresses, my posture, my skin tone, my smile." She threw up her hands, her frustration obviously still fresh. "I was never flirtatious enough. I never caught the eye of the right gentlemen."

"You caught *my* eye."

She made no effort to hide her scoff. "I only truly claimed your attention once I told you of my dowry."

What exactly could he say to that? Emmeline possessed a subtle beauty, not the kind that sparkled in a ballroom, but one that grew with an understanding of her wit, her kindness, her curiosity. Yet if he said as much she would not take it in the complimentary way he intended.

His stateman's mind sorted through possibilities, wanting to ease the sting of past slights. "If she made you feel anything less than beautiful she was—is—a fool. I consider myself fortunate to have secured such an attractive wife. And you can believe me, for I have no obligation to say such things now that your dowry is being used to rebuild Chelten House."

Her dark eyes swirled with doubt. "If you'll excuse me, Lord Anslowe, I am tired from the journey. I think I shall rest before dinner."

He wished she hadn't retreated from their conversation. It was the most personal exchange they'd shared in a year of marriage, and he found he craved more. He bowed his head in acknowledgement. "I'll send someone up to press your things before dinner."

She turned to go.

"Perhaps you'll find you enjoy social settings more as a married woman," he found himself saying.

She straightened but didn't fully look him in the eye. "Perhaps."

CHAPTER 6

*E*mmeline forced her eyes open, blinking against the sunshine streaming through the expansive windows. For a moment she considered barricading herself under the covers. Would Lord Anslowe even notice her absence? No one else would, she was certain.

The headache she'd acquired during dinner last night continued to throb against her temples, as persistent as the waves pounding down at the beach. She was unaccustomed to fashionable hours and the thought of another week's worth of late nights, trivial conversation, and inedible food made Emmeline doubt her wisdom in agreeing to come. If she didn't wish to go abroad so badly she would call for the carriage to take her home this very moment.

Instead, she would call for the carriage and venture into town to seek out some powders for her headache at the apothecary. Not only did she need a remedy for her aching head, but it would be much easier for her to avoid a particular guest she'd discovered at dinner last night. Miss Hastings. The very woman Lord Anslowe would have proposed to if not for Emmeline. And from the shriveling glare she'd received from Miss Hastings, the woman had not forgotten.

The sound of the ocean drew her gaze toward the open window. She finally pulled back the covers and took a seat on the fainting couch that was positioned near the drapes, giving its occupant full advantage of the view.

She had absolutely no desire to go downstairs for breakfast. If she was required to socialize every time she wanted some sustenance, it seemed certain she would waste away during her stay.

When a knock sounded at the door Emmeline pulled her wrap tightly up to her neck. Would Lord Anslowe expect her to accompany him downstairs for breakfast? They hadn't discussed it. But it was Bridget who peeked in, not her husband.

"Believe me when I tell you it isn't worth going downstairs for breakfast. I brought you what little there is. Boiled eggs and toast." She wrinkled her nose as she set the tray down. "And tea so weak it hardly deserves the name."

Emmeline smiled. Her lady's maid had never quite mastered the art of tact.

"What would you like on your toast?"

"Thank you, Bridget. I can butter it myself. Perhaps you could pick out a dress for me and tell me what is planned for the day. I didn't intend to sleep so late." She picked up a piece of toast. The bread was so thin she could almost see through it.

"Lord Anslowe went out for an early morning ride with several of the other gentlemen. There doesn't seem to be a strict schedule." Bridget laughed and opened up the large wardrobe in the corner. "Mostly because there are too many guests for all of them to do anything together. You should see the chaos below stairs. Servants running every which way and Mrs. Daw doing her level best to avoid Mrs. Garvey who is sure to be displeased with anything and everything."

Though she'd met her only briefly, Emmeline liked Mrs. Daw immensely and sympathized with her at the thought of trying to please the formidable Mrs. Garvey. "Poor Mrs. Daw. Mrs. Garvey must be difficult to work with."

Mr. and Mrs. Garvey certainly seemed to be an ill-suited pair. Did everyone think the same about Lord Anslowe and herself? She'd watched him last night, making his rounds through the guests, never lacking for companionship, liberally doling out compliments and leaving smiles in his wake. He was a master at flattery. Which was precisely why she couldn't trust what he'd said to her yesterday. Emmeline wasn't a beauty by any standard, and his saying so provided no evidence to the contrary. He must know that giving compliments so freely only cheapened them.

"A truer fact was never spoken." Bridget's mouth quirked in a mischievous grin. "Though we all enjoy hearing Mrs. Garvey constantly criticizing her husband under her breath."

What had they been discussing? Oh yes, the Garveys. "At least there is that," Emmeline granted with half a smile. "Bridget, I'd like to go into Brighton. Would you like to accompany me?" She wouldn't sit around and wait for her husband.

"Oh yes, my lady. I'd be happy to come. I've always wished to see the ocean up close."

An hour later she and Bridget were in the heart of Brighton. The streets were narrow and quaint, paved with cobblestones and full of tourists. Emmeline and Bridget pushed their way through the crowds.

"It's much newer than London, isn't it?" asked Bridget.

"Yes," Emmeline agreed. Every shop was freshly painted, boasting elaborate window displays to try and lure in potential customers. "The town has very nearly sprung up overnight. I suppose the Prince Regent's renowned Pavilion is responsible for Brighton's newfound popularity."

Bridget gawked at everything and wanted to stop in every shop. Emmeline humored her, since she had no desire to hurry back to Havencrest. They explored a hat shop, several dress shops, and a charming little perfumerie where Bridget talked Emmeline into buying a honey and lavender scented perfume. The scent was sweet and fresh without the cloying smell of so many of the other fragrances.

After leaving an elegant shop with parasols, reticules, and any other accessory a lady might need, Emmeline spotted an apothecary. She quickly ran in and purchased the powders for her headache. As they awaited the carriage to take them back to Havencrest, Emmeline peered across the street to make out a sign that read, *The Bake Shop.*

She tugged on Bridget's arm. "Look, Bridget! We deserve a pastry after the paltry meals we have suffered through. Come!" They bustled across the street, only to find a plump woman setting out a closed sign.

"Can you not sell us something?" Emmeline pleaded.

"I would, madam, but I am all sold out. It's the Garveys' house party. Happens every year. All of the starving guests come straight here."

"I see." Emmeline tried to curb the disappointment of both her sweet tooth and her growling stomach. At last their carriage pulled around the corner. She cast one last longing glance at the bakery, mocked by the smell of warm butter, yeast, and sugar that hung in the air.

Bridget followed her back across the street to the waiting carriage. To her surprise, Lord Anslowe stood there. Emmeline very nearly dropped her reticule. What was her husband doing here? And how had he found her? And why did he have to look so dashing with his long lean frame propped against the carriage looking quite at his leisure?

But before she could question him he smiled, further disarming her. "Ah, there you are."

"Here I am." She battled to keep her voice even. Which was more than difficult when her pulse insisted on galloping forward at an indecent pace.

"Some of the guests are up at the cliffs. I thought you might want to join them."

She pursed her lips together. Of course she wanted to see the cliffs. She'd been hoping for another chance to explore them since she'd gotten the tiniest glimpse from the carriage yesterday. But seeing him, her husband—just being in his presence—set her off kilter. And she didn't want him to think she would be at his beck and call any time he felt like paying her a little attention.

His brow furrowed in response to her silence. "Was I wrong?"

Her desire to explore won out. "No, no. I've been hoping for a chance to see the cliffs."

Lord Anslowe held out his hand. "Well then, let's be off." Her husband was the kind of man who, once he decided upon a course of action, wasted no time in pursuing it. Just as he had when she'd offered to become his wife. She placed her gloved hand in his and he handed her up into the carriage.

Lord Anslowe did not follow. "Come, Bridget." He beckoned, waiting for Emmeline's maid.

"Oh, I cannot join you, my lord. The afternoon is getting on and I should press Lady Anslowe's dress for dinner this evening."

Emmeline peered out the open door. "At least let us take you up to the house. It is right on the way."

Bridget turned to Lord Anslowe. "Might I walk home? I'll enjoy walking up the road near the ocean so much more."

Emmeline was about to object when Lord Anslowe shrugged. "We cannot deny her that, now can we?"

Emmeline very much wished to deny her that. Without Bridget, Emmeline was without a buffer, alone with Lord Anslowe. The very prospect was unsettling.

But with a small wave Bridget was off.

The carriage wheeled along in silence for a moment before Emmeline gathered her thoughts. "How did you know Bridget's name?" she asked.

"She's your abigail, isn't she? You've mentioned her in your letters several times."

The fact that Lord Anslowe remembered what she'd written surprised her. She half expected he didn't take the time to even read her letters. "Oh." Her stomach did an odd flip.

Lord Anslowe stretched his long legs, crossing his boots in a relaxed manner. "The view of the Pavilion is quite breathtaking. Did you have the chance to see the Prince Regent's illustrious new residence while you were out?"

Emmeline clutched her reticule, as if it might anchor her against her tendency to weaken under her husband's charm. "No. We browsed through a few of the shops and then stopped at the apothecary."

"What did you need at the apothecary?"

"I've had a lingering headache since last night. I bought myself some powders to see if they wouldn't help."

His mouth turned downward. "You should have said something. I would have sent someone to fetch them for you."

Emmeline looked away. "You were gone this morning, and I didn't wish to trouble your aunt."

"I am sorry I didn't check on you before leaving this morning. I'm not accustomed to being an attentive husband." He rubbed a hand along his jawline and for a moment Emmeline had the strangest notion of wishing to do the same.

Instead she waved her hand, dismissing his apology. "Lord Anslowe, I am perfectly capable of seeing to my own needs. There's no need for you to pay me any mind."

He leaned across the seat, eliminating most of the space between them. "Emmeline, you are my wife. Of course I must give you the attention you deserve. Even if you are more than capable of looking after yourself." He gave her a wry grin. "A man likes to think himself useful, after all. Now, are you sure you wish to see the cliffs this afternoon? Perhaps it would better suit your headache if you were to rest. The sun reflects off the ocean, and that may only make it worse."

One year ago, upon her marriage to Lord Anslowe, Emmeline had rid herself of a critical mother and any and all attention she had been given. She had taken her newfound independence and wrapped it around herself like a blanket, growing accustomed to solitude, to looking out for herself. Lord Anslowe leaned across the carriage now, elbows on his knees, tugging on that blanket, as if she needed someone to care for her, to coddle her. Tempting as it was to throw caution to the wind and allow herself the luxury of being cared for by someone else, Emmeline knew that after the house party things would go back to the way they were before. She would be left alone and it was best not to grow attached. So she clutched at the comfort of relying only on herself and put on a wide smile. "My headache has all but disappeared."

He nodded, taking her at her word. "Very well." He sat up and tapped on the roof of the carriage, signaling the driver. The ride was short, as the carriage could not take them too far up the sloping hills. They stopped at the side of the road, where the grass-topped knolls led up toward the top of the cliffs. Lord Anslowe helped Emmeline out of the carriage and extended his arm.

They walked in silence for a few moments, both needing their breath as they climbed. There were only a few people wandering at the top of the cliffs. "Did we miss the outing?"

Lord Anslowe glanced up at the sun. "It's almost four. Perhaps so."

"Do you wish to go back?"

"Of course not. You still wish to see the cliffs, don't you?"

"Yes."

"Well, then. Upward and onward."

They ascended at a moderate pace, and Emmeline was grateful her arm was tucked in his, as the gradient hid some uneven footing that nearly caused her to trip. They crested the hill where the ocean came into view and Emmeline stopped, her breath catching. Sunlight sparkled over the expanse of turquoise ocean. To their left, the sheer crags jutted up toward the sky in majestic glory, the rock cliffs as white as pearls. It all came together in a way that was too beautiful for words.

The wind played with loose strands of her hair, and Lord Anslowe leaned toward her, his gentle fingers brushing her hair back. "Perhaps now you do not regret accompanying me to this house party."

"No," she breathed.

He chuckled low. "Perhaps I should be offended, but I am not. I used to come here every summer as a boy. And even though I've seen this view hundreds of times, the look of awe on your face captures my feelings exactly."

"'One touch of nature makes the whole world kin,'" Emmeline quoted softly, still unable to tear away her gaze.

"Ah, you are a lover of Shakespeare as well as cliffs."

She glanced over at Lord Anslowe, whose eyes were soft, reflecting back the light of the ocean. "I am."

"And do you enjoy novels as well?"

"Sometimes, though most cannot compete with the lyricism of Shakespeare. The cadence and rhythm of poetry is what I truly love."

He gave her an appraising look and then nodded. "I enjoy poetry as well. I have always revered the power of words. It is one of the things I love about politics, I think. The necessity of crafting words in such a way that makes people listen."

"It shows. Everyone listens when you speak." Her voice was a little too breathless. But the thought of sharing a love of words, of poetry, felt strangely intimate.

He cocked his head a little, as if surprised at her admission. "I should hope so. I *am* Viscount Anslowe, after all." He winked at her, and Emmeline's heart thudded in her chest, suddenly louder than the waves below or the slight howl of the wind that inhabited the cliffs. "You're not afraid of heights are you?" he asked.

"No."

He gave her one of those arrogant grins, crease lines bracketing the sides of his mouth. "Then come with me. When you stand near the edge and look down on the ocean, it feels as though you are at the top of the world."

CHAPTER 7

"*B*ut England is still feeling the effects of last summer's poor crops. Tenants everywhere are barely scraping by. And if they suffer, so will we." Lord Tyndale's mouth was drawn in a firm line, his arms crossed over his chest.

Lord Bellamy picked up his port, swirling the liquid. "And what would you have us do? Farmers have weathered the ups and downs of the land many a time. They will do so again, and without our help."

Tyndale turned to Anslowe. "Lord Anslowe, what do you think?"

Anslowe uncrossed his legs as he gathered his thoughts. "It's a difficult matter to be sure. One thing is certain, our country is in a precarious state. Our years at war with Napoleon drained our treasury, depleted our resources, and exhausted our army and navy. Somehow it doesn't seem right to ignore the plight of the very men who helped us claim victory in Europe. But how to help them? I'd hoped to meet with Prinny to discuss a new bill that addresses the needs of those who have been most affected by these hardships."

Bellamy's mouth curled up in a smirk. "Prinny is too busy eating and drinking and enjoying his new abode to be interested in such matters."

"Well, we must make him take interest then," said Tyndale.

Bellamy set down his empty glass. "You are welcome to try. I, for one, am heading to bed. It's too late to be discussing such serious matters."

Anslowe glanced around the room, only now noticing the room had emptied out. Emmeline must have retired without him. He felt a stab of guilt for neglecting her.

"I think you are right," he conceded, getting to his feet. The clock on the mantle claimed the hour as half past one. The men slowly dispersed, but Anslowe's head was still full of their discussion. There was little consensus on how to rebuild after long years at war. Usually political talk invigorated him, but tonight he felt drained. He trudged up the stairs.

When he reached his corridor, he found Aunt Garvey snuffing out candles. "Nonsensical waste," she muttered. "Loose screw Garvey."

"Good evening, Aunt Garvey."

Her pinched face turned toward him. "Don't 'Aunt Garvey' me. You have no respect. You stay up late, burning candles, drinking our port, running my modest budget into the ground."

The Garveys could throw a hundred such house parties without a care for the cost, but nothing would convince Aunt Garvey of that. Anslowe pulled at his cravat. "I brought my own candles, so you can hardly fault me for that."

"It is still a waste," she said. "You should be in bed. With your *wife*," she said pointedly. "It's no wonder she's off gallivanting with Lord Wembley with the way you hardly pay her a fig's worth of attention."

"Aunt Garvey—"

"He's in Brighton, you know."

Anslowe's head whipped up, finally giving her his full attention.

"Ah, you didn't know," she said, a tad too gleefully. "Perhaps you'll think twice before you ignore your wife for an entire evening again. Good night, Lord Anslowe." She emphasized *Lord* in an almost mocking tone, then moved down the hallway without a backward glance.

Anslowe quickened his pace, striding toward his rooms with determination. A large rock had settled in his stomach, just thinking of Emmeline with Lord Wembley. It couldn't be. Surely she was in bed. He'd check on her, just to be certain. It was no more than any husband would do.

He pushed open the door. The small sitting area was empty. Despite his agitation, he crossed the room quietly and silently pulled down the handle that led to Emmeline's room. He nudged the door open with care. The darkness made it difficult to see so Anslowe held his candle up, only to find that the bed remained undisturbed. Emmeline's night clothes were laid out over the coverlet, a white gauzy material lined with lace.

"Emmeline?" he called. No answer.

The rock in his stomach turned to nausea. He ran a hand through his hair and scrubbed it down his face. Behind him a slight creak sounded. He whirled around to find Emmeline sneaking into the room, looking for all the world like a thief in the night. Her eyes shone bright even in the candlelight and a flush painted her cheeks a warm pink.

"Lord Anslowe!" she squeaked.

"Where have you been?" he demanded.

Her eyes flew wide, guilt written clearly across her face. "I—I...I was down in the kitchen." She swallowed. "With Mrs. Daw."

She was a very poor liar, using the housekeeper of all people as her alibi. "With Mrs. Daw?" He made no effort to hide his skepticism.

"Y-yes." One hand rested behind her back and she shifted, as if to hide something. "And Lady Felicity." Her chin rose in defiance.

"And what were you doing with the two of them, pray tell?"

"We were talking."

"Talking?" he challenged.

Emmeline shifted uncomfortably. "And eating...biscuits. Mrs. Daw sent me up with some extra." A pause ensued, and she pulled a small tin from behind her back. "She told me to share with you, but..." She bit her lip, a sheepish grin turning up the corners of her mouth. "I selfishly considered saving them all for myself."

Anslowe released the breath he'd been holding, and the tension that had been cramping his limbs eased away. His wife had been guilty of sneaking biscuits, nothing more. Shame swept through him, though Emmeline didn't know what he'd suspected her of.

"You weren't going to share?" he teased.

She ducked her head. "Well, I suppose now I must."

With only the soft halo of the candle giving light to the room, and Emmeline standing there, her skin a creamy white against the dark curls that framed her face, his thoughts drifted, wondering what it would be like to be husband and wife in truth. Anslowe glanced at the bed, all at once feeling the full impact of their proximity.

Emmeline followed his gaze and blushed as she caught sight of her night rail. She handed him the tin. "I should get to bed."

But he wasn't willing to let her go, not yet. His aunt was right. He *was* a fool for being so careless, so inattentive. Curse their wretched bargain. "No," he said softly. "Not yet. Won't you sit with me for a few minutes?" He gestured toward the door, toward the sitting room that connected their bedrooms.

"I—" Confusion marred her dark brow. For a moment it seemed she would protest, but the line of her jaw softened. "A few minutes, I suppose. On one condition." Then her mouth twisted into a playful expression Anslowe had never seen before. Taking him by surprise, she snatched the tin back from his hands. "The biscuits are mine." She retreated to the sitting room before he could react.

By the time Anslowe had regained his faculties and followed her, she sat on the small sofa and had opened the tin. She bit into one of the biscuits and gave a little moan. "I've been practically starved the last few days, you know."

"Aunt Garvey isn't exactly known for her lavish dinners," he agreed. "But tonight we ate well, you must admit." Anslowe took a seat in the chair beside her, trying to come to terms with this new and bewitching side to the woman who was his wife. She reached for another biscuit, acting as if she couldn't tell how badly he wanted one.

"Only because Mr. Garvey was there. Perhaps he only makes appearances so his guests won't starve to death." She brushed a crumb from her lip, and suddenly Anslowe didn't want a biscuit anymore. He wanted to take the tin from Emmeline's lap, pull her to him, and kiss her. Soundly.

But he tamped down the impulse. He wasn't willing to scare her away, not when this was the first time she had truly let down her guard. "Aren't you going to share even one?" he asked.

"Tell me what topic so thoroughly captured your attention this evening and I'll consider it. The debate amongst you gentlemen sounded fierce." She fixed her gaze upon him, as if she really did wish to know.

"We were discussing the desperate struggle so many of the tenant farmers are facing after last year's weather. And with so many sons lost or maimed in the war." He shook his head, still a little despondent.

"I know several of our tenants are facing that very thing. I have tried to give extra where I can, but they are proud. They don't want charity." She set down her half-eaten biscuit. "Something must be done, surely."

"Something, yes. But it is a controversial matter. Our country's finances have been depleted by years at war."

Resolve glinted in Emmeline's eyes. "England cannot turn her back on the very men who won her the war."

The immediacy with which she responded, the conviction in her tone took Anslowe aback. He'd never truly considered discussing politics with a woman, or his own wife for that matter, yet he found her eloquent. Passionate. "I am glad to know we share the same views."

She blushed prettily, then reached into the tin and handed him a biscuit. Her soft, slender fingers brushed his and his heart tripped at the brief contact. "So, what is to be done?" she asked. "I know the plight of those in Wales and Ireland is particularly bad."

Anslowe imagined for a moment what it would be like to have Emmeline by his side, to have her support and encouragement, even her voice alongside his as he navigated those topics about which he was most passionate. Something in the vicinity of his heart swelled. "I'd hoped to gain Prinny's ear while we are here in Brighton to discuss this very thing," he said quietly. "And Lord Sotheby. If I can convince him to support my bill, it may well have a chance."

"You are here for politics? Why did you not say so?" Her bottom lip jutted out. "For a matter of such importance I would have been willing to support your endeavors."

Her words brought one hard truth to the forefront of his mind. If Emmeline was seeing Lord Wembley, her very actions could undermine his position in Parliament, making it impossible for him to accomplish his aims. For a moment he considered confessing the truth in its entirety. But how could he, when she would surely take it as a blatant accusation? If the rumors were not true—and he was beginning to doubt them—he would alienate the very woman he was beginning to care for. He simply couldn't do it.

"I had not thought you would take an interest," he finally said. It was the truth.

"Yes, well." She cleared her throat. "Perhaps I shall give you more than you bargained for."

One way or another, he was quite sure that was true.

CHAPTER 8

*O*n Wednesday, the skies opened and rain poured down steadily outside the windows. No doubt the entirety of the house party would be confined within the walls of Havencrest today. As Emmeline was leaving her room to head downstairs, she caught sight of the tin of biscuits. With a furtive glance she opened the tin and pulled out two biscuits. She took a bite. The taste was heavenly, full of ginger and cinnamon.

"Biscuits for breakfast?"

Emmeline startled and whirled around, dropping one of the biscuits in the process.

Lord Anslowe stood in the doorway, an amused expression on his face.

"You scared me half to death!" She frowned at the crumbled biscuit on the rug.

He only laughed as he headed for the door. "Do you look guilty because you are eating biscuits for breakfast or because you weren't planning to share?"

"Both." Emmeline took a bite.

"I should have expected as much. And what are your plans for the morning?"

"I have plans to meet Lady Felicity to do some needlework."

"Ah, well enjoy yourself. And be sure to wash your hands before you go." He winked. "Wouldn't want to get crumbs on your stitching." With a bow of the head he was gone.

Emmeline smoothed her skirts, feeling quite undone. It was fortunate he didn't spend much time with her, otherwise her cheeks might be stained with a permanent blush.

She headed downstairs and made the requisite appearances as the ladies gathered in the drawing rooms, mostly mixing with those who were young and unmarried.

Her mind wandered, drifting to the unexpected time she'd spent with her husband the night before. She'd been utterly surprised by his desire to sit and talk with her. Her stomach twirled and somersaulted all over again as she relived the memory.

Had he enjoyed their time together as she had? Though her husband had a charming exterior, she relished seeing his sharp mind work and appreciated the depth of his concern for the state of the country. So many gentlemen seemed interested in nothing more than fashion, riding and shooting. Or like her own father, in trade, who only concerned himself with making money. How she wished he wouldn't dabble in speculation.

After discovering Lady Felicity was abed with a fever, Emmeline excused herself. She gathered her writing materials and made her way to the library, determined to cheer up her new friend with a kind note. While there, she stumbled across Lord Bolton, who intended to take Lady Felicity something as well, and quickly agreed to deliver Emmeline's note with his offering. Emmeline smiled, imagining him teasing her proper friend. She would have to question Lady Felicity about the handsome Lord Bolton the next time their paths crossed.

She passed the afternoon in her room with her book and a much-needed nap. Other guests seemed unphased by the late hours of the house party, but Emmeline still yawned through the long evenings.

Bridget helped her change her dress before dinner and she made her way out into the hall when Lord Anslowe came upon her, handsome as ever with his light brown hair falling across his forehead.

He turned the full power of his smile upon her. "There you are! I thought perhaps you'd been spirited away in the storm."

"Oh no. The rain always makes me wish to curl up with a book and I fell fast asleep. Thank goodness Bridget woke me, or I might have slept through dinner and offended your aunt and uncle."

He tipped back his head and laughed. "You'll soon learn that Aunt Garvey chooses to be offended by everything and Uncle Garvey by nothing, so you needn't fear on their accounts."

"All the same, we should make our way downstairs. I don't want to be late."

He tucked her hand into his arm and escorted her downstairs. The thrill of his nearness had Emmeline scolding herself. How silly for her to be so easily affected by her husband.

Before they were separated to take their seats at the table, Lord Anslowe leaned down and spoke directly in her ear. "Come find me tonight, before you retire." His gaze stayed on her far longer than necessary and Emmeline grew warm all over.

After dinner, Miss Lucy Brook took a seat next to her in the drawing room. Though they'd spoken only a few times, Emmeline liked her a great deal. She was clever and independent, a wealthy heiress who presided over a bank. And while Miss Brook was quite pretty, it was the self-assurance she possessed that Emmeline envied.

Several other ladies joined them, including Aunt Garvey. The women began discussing the advantages and disadvantages of marriage, and Emmeline stayed mostly silent, answering only when directly asked a question.

The conversation moved on, but Miss Brook leaned in. "I hope this is not impertinent to ask, but I'm curious to know. Did you marry for love or more practical reasons?"

From someone else the question may well have been impertinent. But Miss Brook didn't seem the type to gossip, and Emmeline instinctively felt as though she could trust her. "I wish I could have married for love," she whispered. "Lord Anslowe married me for one reason— my dowry." She brushed back a strand of her hair.

Miss Brook reached out a hand and clasped Emmeline's. "That

cannot be. I have observed the two of you together. The way he looks at you . . ." She nodded. "Surely Lord Anslowe has come to care for you."

How badly Emmeline wished that were true. And for a few moments last night she'd hoped... "But how could I ever truly know?" she asked Miss Brook. Her dowry would always cast a long shadow between them.

"I am not certain," admitted Miss Brook. "But I believe it is a possibility he may come to care for you deeply."

Emmeline squeezed Miss Brook's hand. True or not, the woman's sincerity meant a great deal to her. The door to the drawing room opened, and the men paraded in. She silently rejoiced when Mr. Garvey walked over and invited Emmeline and Miss Brook to join in a card game, so she would have something other than her troublesome husband to focus on.

Captain Sharpe, a young and handsome naval captain, rounded out the foursome and Emmeline immediately sensed attraction between him and Miss Brook. The two of them partnered, while she was paired with Mr. Garvey, which made for quite a mismatched game. It was a long, drawn-out hour of continual defeat.

"Well, they've beaten us soundly, Lady Anslowe. I always say that is the cue for our exit." Mr. Garvey rose and extended his hand toward Emmeline. As soon as he'd helped her to her feet, he bounded off.

Emmeline began to laugh and Captain Sharpe and Miss Brook joined in. Mr. Garvey was quite a character. As their laughter petered out, Emmeline inclined her head. "I'm afraid I must concede to your superior abilities in whist," she said. "And since I am denied my energetic partner, I will go in search of my husband." She gave Miss Brook a broad smile as she turned away, leaving Captain Sharpe to admire her friend in a more intimate setting.

The room was crowded and boisterous. For such a late hour, the guests seemed nowhere near retiring. Emmeline stayed near the far wall as she searched for Lord Anslowe. Despite what he'd said earlier, she felt almost presumptuous seeking him out. Did he only wish to say goodnight? Or would he accompany her back to their rooms?

Finally she caught sight of him, standing in a circle of gentlemen. He looked over and caught her eye. He pursed his lips together, then held up a finger. She nodded, willing to wait.

A few feet to her right sat a semi-circle of women, including Miss Hastings. Emmeline angled herself back behind the large arrangement of flowers that decorated the table between them. She had no desire to be drawn into that conversation. But she couldn't help but overhear her name.

"Have you not seen how little time Lord and Lady Anslowe spend in one another's company? No doubt she has grown tired of her husband's lack of attention." Miss Tittering raised her eyebrows and lowered her voice. "It is said she has been seen a great deal in the company of Lord Wembley."

"Who is this Lord Wembley?" asked Lady Tyndale.

"Why he is Lord Anslowe's political foe," answered Miss Tittering. "What a way for a wife to have her revenge."

Miss Hastings uttered a derisive scoff. "That is ridiculous. Everyone knows the woman is so cold she drives her own husband away. It is obvious why she hasn't yet produced an heir—he wants nothing to do with her."

Emmeline pressed a hand over her mouth to cover the gasp that nearly escaped. Humiliation burned her cheeks and the scornful words echoed through her head. *Everyone knows she is so cold she drives her own husband away.* She stumbled backward, intent on fleeing before anyone bore witness to her mortification. As she turned she ran straight into Lord Anslowe's chest.

She took a step back, trying to right herself and put distance between them. He placed a hand on her shoulder, steadying her. One glance told her he'd heard everything. His left brow quirked down, hinting at regret, but also uncertainty.

Her chin quivered, and she could not even look him in the eye. Was *this* what everyone thought of her? What *he* thought? And had her own husband known what was being said?

She pushed away from him, heading toward the door of the

drawing room. A moment later footsteps sounded behind her, but she didn't slow, didn't stop. How could she ever face him again?

"Emmeline, wait!"

She reached the banister and mounted the steps as quickly as she could without tripping on her skirts. At the top of the stairs Lord Anslowe pulled even with her. She broke into a run, sprinting down the hall, not even sparing him a glance. Tears threatened, but she wouldn't cry in front of him. If only she could reach the sanctuary of her room.

"Emmeline, please." Her husband's voice was soft, entreating.

She burst through the doorway of the sitting room and headed straight for her room. In one swift move she opened her door, turned, but before she could close it and bolt herself in, he wedged his boot in front of it. "I need to speak with you."

He made no move to push his way in but left his boot in place. She tried to catch her breath for a moment, blood rushing to her skull and making her a bit light headed. She needed time and space to think, to sort through this awful mess she'd unwittingly walked into.

Something thumped softly against the door. Lord Anslowe's head perhaps. "Please."

An unexpected surge of anger shot through her. *Now* he wanted to talk? Now that her name was fuel for the fire around which gossipers congregated? Hoping to take him by surprise, she wrenched the door open. Lord Anslowe's head jerked back and he nearly lost his footing. "Did you know?" she demanded. She stepped forward, toe to toe with him.

His eyes darkened.

"The rumors. Did you know about them before we came?"

His mouth thinned into a firm line. "I knew the rumors about you and Lord Wembley, yes."

Her lip trembled but she bit into it, fighting against any show of weakness. "And this is what everyone believes of me? You should have warned me. Even if we do not live as husband and wife, you owed me that much! How could you let me come here, unprepared against such an onslaught?" Her chest heaved.

"It was wrong of me, Emmeline. I should have warned you." His voice was tight.

The apology did little to assuage her mortification. "And do you believe the rumors?" Tears hovered, threatening to spill over any moment.

He raked a hand through his hair. "I don't know."

She stepped back, surprisingly gutted by his lack of faith in her. "And this is your opinion of me?" she whispered.

He reached out and took hold of her just above the elbows. "Devil take it woman, I don't know you well enough to *have* an opinion of you! You've been dead-set on keeping me at arm's length."

"I have done nothing more than what we agreed upon," she protested. A tear slipped down her cheek.

"Ah, yes. Our bargain." He blew out a breath, then abruptly let her go and crossed to one of the sofas. He sat down heavily. "I made a mistake when you approached me a year ago, Emmeline."

His words snaked around her like the end of a whip, biting into her, slicing through her heart. She lifted a hand to cover her mouth before a sob could escape. But he was oblivious, hunched over his knees, staring at his boots. "I did us both a disservice when I agreed to your proposal. I was distracted with the approaching parliamentary session. You offered so much and demanded so little. How could I argue or protest when you so willingly presented yourself and the money with which to repair Chelten House? You at least deserved to set the terms of our arrangement."

Her eyes flew open. "Are you unhappy with our arrangement?" She hated how her hands shook as she waited for him to answer.

"I know you married me to escape your mother. And I married you for your dowry. Not the best start, by any account." He returned her question with one of his own. "But have you ever hoped there might be more between us?"

"Lord Anslowe—"

He gave a brief shake of the head, cutting her off. "Not Lord Anslowe. Just plain Anslowe, if you please. We are married, after all." The irony in his voice was thick.

"Anslowe—" His name came out stilted, felt far too familiar. "Of course I wish for more," she said softly. "But I fear it, too." Her throat bobbed.

He looked up, his brown eyes dull and shadowed. "I don't wish for a business partner, Emmeline. Or someone who runs the estate in my absence. I don't want this sham of a marriage."

Emmeline's ribcage constricted, making it nearly impossible to draw in a full breath of air. What was he saying? "A sham? Because I drive you away? Because we...keep our separate rooms?"

"Forget what that hateful woman said—our sleeping arrangements are the least of my worries. I wish to know you, as I ought to have done from the beginning."

The anguish twisting itself around her heart eased a bit.

"I don't want to wait another four years, Emmeline. I want to court you and become acquainted with you." He straightened and let out a breath, his chest falling.

"And then?" she asked. Dared she hope that he might want what she had always wished for?

He got up from the sofa and crossed the room to where she stood. Her knees trembled as he closed the distance between them. "And I hope we can come to admire and respect one another, to live together as husband and wife—without any secrets between us." He met her gaze, his expression soft and vulnerable. "I hope that we will come to love each another."

She paused mid-breath, her lips parted. His words, the way they made her feel—it was so very much like standing on the edge of Brighton's cliffs. Heady and reckless and daring. But the chance of falling, the deep plunge to the rocky shores below—terrifying.

"May we try?" he asked, expectation lifting his voice.

She could barely hear her own voice above the thundering of her heart. "Yes." She nodded. "Yes, I think I would like to try." A prick of joy pulsed through her chest.

Anslowe reached out, and his fingers drifted ever so softly down her neck. He leaned in, his whisper a caress across her cheek. "I do not imagine it will be very hard to fall in love with you."

CHAPTER 9

*A*nslowe listened for the click of Emmeline's door before he allowed himself to grin like a fool. He'd almost kissed her. Standing so close to her, the intoxicating smell of her skin and the rosy hue that enlivened her cheeks had made it almost impossible for him to resist.

But now was not the time for giving into impulsive behavior. Something made her hesitant about opening herself up to love, even to him, her husband. Perhaps something from her past had taught her that love was not to be trusted.

And so he would, as with anything that mattered to him, take his time.

Anslowe retreated to his room and shut the door behind him, electing not to ring for his valet and instead undress himself. He unknotted his cravat, frowning as he remembered the look of anguish upon her face as she'd overheard her name being bandied about as fodder for gossip. Anger boiled beneath his skin, at the women who had spoken so thoughtlessly. Though he'd given Miss Hastings a set down, how he wished he could have done more.

But deep down, Anslowe was angry with himself. He'd been selfish. He'd thought only of his own image and had given no thought to how such rumors might affect Emmeline. What a cad he was. He finished undressing and climbed into bed, but it was a long time before sleep pulled him under.

Despite the pattering of rain against the window that awoke him the next morning, Anslowe couldn't bring himself to be put out with another day of stormy weather. He rose with a sense of purpose. He'd spent nearly an hour last night planning and strategizing how best to court his wife. And there were a few things that required his immediate attention.

Once he'd sent off a brief missive, he called for his valet and quickly dressed, anxious to get a start on the day. As he stepped from his bedroom into the small sitting room he caught Bridget as she let herself out of Emmeline's room.

"Bridget, a word with you, if I may." He kept his voice low and motioned for her to step away from the door.

"Certainly, my lord."

"I know it is Lady Anslowe's birthday this week. Would you happen to know which day?"

"It's on Saturday, my lord."

He nodded. "Very good. One more thing. I sent down to the bakery in town for some pastries and they should be arriving any minute. Would you run downstairs to collect the delivery and set it on a tray?"

Her eyes grew round. "Oh yes!"

"Thank you." He pulled out the folded paper he'd composed just a few minutes earlier. "See that this is placed on the tray, alongside the pastries."

EMMELINE SAT AT HER VANITY, reliving each word she and Anslowe had spoken to one another the night before. She felt strangely jittery, on edge even as she waited for Bridget to bring her breakfast tray. With Anslowe's promise to court her and their agreement to try and form a real attachment, she could hardly think straight.

She nearly jumped when Bridget pushed open the door. Bridget's hands were occupied with a heavily laden tray, piled high with delectable-looking pastries and perfectly formed scones. A pot of chocolate let out a small cloud of steam. Emmeline's mouth grew round.

As if sensing her thoughts, Bridget smiled. "Lord Anslowe sent down to the bakery in Brighton for your breakfast." She set the tray down, oblivious to the way Emmeline's stomach turned over at such a thoughtful gesture.

Bridget gave her a sly look. "And I heard about what he did last night."

"Last night?"

"What he said to Miss Hastings, who was being all nasty-like."

Emmeline's heart was suddenly in her throat. "What did he say?"

Bridget's eyes grew round. "He gave her quite the set down, from what I heard. Told her she didn't know of what she was speaking and warned her not to mention your name again."

He must have said something once she'd left the room. Emmeline pressed a hand to her stomach. It was difficult to fathom someone standing up for her. And for that someone to be her husband... She pursed her lips together, her heart swelling at the unexpected gesture.

Her eye caught a small paper in the corner of the tray, simply marked -E-. Careful not to bump the mountain of pastries, she reached for the note and unfolded it.

Emmeline,

I should have thought to do this sooner, but I cannot allow you to waste away from hunger. Hopefully now there will be no need for you to eat biscuits for breakfast.

There's to be a fencing tournament this afternoon. I'd be pleased if you would meet me down in the library to spend some time together this morning, and then we can attend the tournament together.

Your husband, A

Her heart tripped seeing the words *your husband*, almost as if he were reminding her.

"Is something amusing, my lady?" Bridget gave her a pert grin.

"I am just relieved with the knowledge I will not starve today. I must insist you join me." Emmeline picked up a flower shaped delicacy with raspberries in each petal and set it on her plate. "I'll hardly make a dent in this mountain of deliciousness."

Bridget's stomach rumbled just then and the two of them broke into laughter. "I suppose my stomach has answered for me," she said, taking a scone for herself.

Once she'd finished breakfast, Emmeline took more care than usual with her appearance. After some deliberation she chose a pale green gown with tiny embroidered white flowers. Bridget did a more elaborate hairstyle, twisting and looping, and leaving several curls framing her face.

And yet, her nerves persisted even as she pushed open the door to the library. Lord Anslowe sat in a deep brown leather chair not far from the door and he got to his feet before she had fully entered the room. "Good morning, Emmeline. I trust you are well."

He looked so hopeful as she approached. Emmeline's heart rose nearly to her throat. "I am, thank you Lor—Anslowe." The familiarity of using his name brought a blush to her cheeks. "There is something I should have told you last night, and I wish to say it now, so that we may," she waved her hand awkwardly, "move forward with nothing between us."

He nodded.

"I only wished to tell you that there is naught between Lord Wembley and I. We met at a dinner party several months ago, but we were never even alone together. It is difficult for me to understand where those rumors might have come from."

"I'm sorry I gave any credence to them." There was contrition in the set of his mouth.

Emmeline hugged her midsection. "I would never do anything to jeopardize your political career."

Anslowe reached for her hand and led her to a settee. "I know you wouldn't. Which is what makes this all the harder." He cleared his throat, for once looking a bit uncomfortable.

Whatever did he mean? The breakfast she'd eaten with such delight an hour before now churned in her stomach.

"I hope you will not misunderstand me. I believe what you said about Lord Wembley." He paused. "Someone mentioned you were alone in the library with Lord Bolton yesterday morning."

Hearing what he left unsaid, she tensed, her knuckles turning white. "I assure you, it was a chance meeting. He agreed to take a note to Lady Felicity for me. That is all."

He raised a hand. "I believe you. I only beg your caution. I have much on the line in this approaching session. Any more rumors and my reputation, my influence, could wane. I will be unable to drum up the necessary votes for my bill. We must be on our guard and do our best to undermine the credibility of scandal."

"Of course." She bowed her head.

"Have you any idea where these circulating rumors might have come from?"

She bit her lip. "I have no proof, but I know of only one person who might hold something against me. Miss Hastings."

"Miss Hastings? Why ever would she do such a thing?"

"You don't remember, do you?" Emmeline felt a little surge of satisfaction at that.

He shook his head, forehead furrowed.

"Were it not for me, I believe you would have offered for her. She must despise me."

He rubbed his brow as understanding stole across his features. "Ah, you are right. I'd forgotten." He grinned at Emmeline, which was not what she'd expected. "Well, I shall consider myself lucky. For not only is she a bore and a gossip, but her teeth are truly awful."

A laugh escaped, nearly a giggle.

Anslowe squeezed her hand. "Hopefully our presence here will lay all the rumors to rest and we will leave people nothing more to discuss than how often Viscount Anslowe has been seen in the company of his very lovely wife."

She gave him a timid smile. "If we are truly to set the tongues wagging, you should have joined me and shared in the lovely breakfast you had sent up. It was too much for one person."

She blushed again at her own boldness. Was she making a fool of herself?

"If you'd like that, perhaps I could. Tomorrow." There was a look of satisfaction upon his face that softened her, made her want to put away her guardedness and just *be*.

"I would like that." It felt like a step had been taken, and some of the tension between them dissipated. Emmeline took in a breath and allowed herself to breathe.

"I don't know if you've heard," Anslowe said, "but supposedly some of the guests will be performing some scenes from *Taming of the Shrew* this evening. Do you have any interest in being a part of the production?"

"Goodness, no." Emmeline gave an emphatic shake of her head. "I have never much enjoyed being the center of attention. But do not feel as though you cannot take part. I would enjoy watching you."

"No, I only thought to ask because you quoted Shakespeare the other day."

"Are you sure? It seems like something you would excel in."

Anslowe considered for a moment. "I would enjoy sitting beside you more. If I had to guess, the whole affair will be quite absurd and the acting will leave much to be desired. Perhaps we could sit near Aunt Garvey and hear her commentary."

Emmeline laughed at that. "A comedy from every angle." He chuckled too, and her toes curled. It frightened her a little. How very easily she might lose her heart to this man she called husband.

CHAPTER 10

The following afternoon Anslowe stood out on the back lawn amongst a growing crowd. Guests milled about, entertained by a variety of lawn games. He mostly watched, enjoying the sun, occasionally being called upon for conversation. The house guests, desperate to be outside despite the muddy field conditions, were noisy and exuberant.

He'd seen Emmeline out walking with Miss Brook earlier, and he surveyed the lawn, hoping for a glimpse of her. There. He spotted her soft pink gown over near the games of battledore. Screams and yelps, shouts of encouragement carried to his ears. After several days of rain, nothing could deter the guests from enjoying the sunny blue skies.

He stayed quiet as he drew closer, glad for a chance to admire her pretty figure before she noticed him. She stood a few feet back from the other guests who were watching a game of battledore. The sun shone behind her, limning her in warm rays of gold. Her lips were pursed in concentration, and her bright eyes followed the quick movement of the game.

When he was only a few feet away, Emmeline looked up, then glanced behind her, as if he might be looking for someone else.

He hated how she'd clearly been taught to doubt herself, which in turn seemed to make her doubt that his care for her might be genuine. No doubt her dragon of a mother had something to do with it.

He bowed his head in greeting. "Would you care to join me for a walk down by the ocean?"

"A proper lady might normally demure, worried about the state of her shoes or the hem of her dress." She held up the mud-caked hem of her skirts with a sigh. "But as the mud has already ruined mine I should be glad to join you."

"Then in this instance I shall be glad for the mud." He offered her his arm and they set off at a leisurely pace.

"Why did you not join in the games?" he asked.

"I prefer to watch. I cannot stand to have so many eyes upon me." She pulled her bottom lip through her teeth. "Does that displease you?"

"Of course not. Why would you think so?"

"You seem to enjoy attention. Or at least, it doesn't bother you. But I am hardly a wife who will be helpful in your many political ambitions."

"I can secure my own ambitions, I assure you. But you do not give yourself enough credit. Your mind is informed and you speak quite eloquently. You are sure to garner respect wherever you go."

They'd reached the steep incline where the path led down to the beach and she gripped his arm more firmly. Despite her bonnet, the sun had managed to tinge her cheeks an attractive pink.

"I saw you with Miss Brook earlier. Has she become a good friend, then?"

"She has. Which reminds me, I was hoping I might ask a favor of you."

The look on her face was so hesitant, so troubled, he wished to reach out and smooth her worry away. "If there is any way possible for me to do it, I will see to it."

She gave him a half smile. "You don't even know what I'm going to ask yet." A mild wind set her bonnet strings flapping.

"Yet I know it pleases me to make you happy."

She ducked her head, but a smile lifted her cheeks. "Miss Brook has become acquainted with Captain Sharpe. Do you know him?"

"Only by reputation." They'd reached the bottom of the path. The sandy beach stretched before them, but Anslowe stopped and turned toward his wife, giving her his full attention.

"He is concerned about the upcoming court martial of some naval officers. I don't know all of the particulars, but he fears they will hang. As I know that you are on the Naval Appropriations Committee, I thought perhaps you might be able to help him somehow, or at least offer him a word of advice."

Concerning all matters regarding the estate, Emmeline was strictly self-sufficient. Even on his occasional visits, Anslowe often felt superfluous. That she would come to him for such a matter gratified him.

She continued on. "I know you are busy and have a great many obligations, but the matter is urgent. If you could at least—"

"Emmeline." He set a finger on her lips, hushing her. "Consider it done."

"Thank you." She stood up on her tiptoes and tentatively leaned toward him. Lit by the reflection of the turquoise ocean, her eyes sparkled. The scent of her filled him, lavender and honey, mixed with the salty ocean breeze. She brushed a kiss across his cheek. Her lips were as soft as rose petals, and his skin heated beneath her touch.

As she began to pull back, he caught her around the waist, keeping her in place. His pulse thrummed with the curve of her hip beneath his hand. He gazed at her, distinctly aware of so many details—the subtle angle of her cheek, that her brows were a shade darker than her hair, the tiny scar on the bridge of her nose. He wanted nothing more than to take her fully in his arms. Her eyes were wide but inviting, so he held himself in check and proceeded cautiously. His hand tightened around her and her lashes fluttered for a moment before she closed her eyes.

He brought his other hand to her cheek and skimmed his lips over the corner of her mouth. She tensed a bit under his touch but didn't pull back. Her unassuming manner, the utter pureness she exuded— he could hardly believe he had given any weight to those malicious rumors. He wanted to make it up to her, to prove himself as someone worthy of a woman such as her. She was sweet and tender. Precious.

She had a tantalizingly full lower lip that urged him closer. He moved his thumb over her cheek and her lips parted on a sigh. At that he was lost. His lips brushed over hers, like a shadow, a promise of more to come.

A high-pitched squeal followed by giggles made him pull back abruptly. Emmeline's eyes grew wide and she quickly turned her head. He nearly cursed at the lost opportunity.

But it was impossible to do anything but smile at the little boy and girl chasing down the sandy shore. Emmeline laughed, dispelling the awkwardness, adjusting her bonnet as she watched them.

"Such carefree joy," he observed.

Emmeline nodded, a gentle smile raising her lips.

"Have you always wanted children?" Genuine curiosity motivated his question.

She stiffened, tight lines appearing around her mouth. "No, my lord."

Was it the thought of starting a family with him that had affected such a change in her behavior? Or did she really not want children?

The boy and girl slowed their chase as they approached, both winded, cheeks rosy red. "Hello," called the little boy in a breathy voice.

Emmeline stepped forward, the earlier tension whisked away. "Hello, who are you?"

"Tim. I'm three." He spoke with a slight lisp and struggled to hold down his pinky with his thumb to show her.

"You're a very big boy." She turned toward the girl. "And who are you?"

"Emma." The girl stayed back behind her brother. She was perhaps five.

Emmeline clapped her hands together. "And my name is Emmeline, which is very close to yours."

The girl gave her a shy smile.

Emmeline touched his elbow. "And this is my husband, Anslowe."

The way she said *my husband* gave him a swell of unexpected pleasure. "Where are your parents?" asked Anslowe.

Tim pointed behind them. "Our nurse is coming. But she can't run very fast." Sure enough, a plump older woman with graying hair waddled along the shoreline. If she was concerned her subjects had gotten so far ahead, she didn't seem it.

"Shall we play a game while we wait for her to catch up?" asked Emmeline. "It's a game I used to play as a girl."

Anslowe watched her with interest, anxious for some insight into her past.

She bent down in front of Tim and Emma. "First, we must gather some shells and rocks. Will you help me?" All traces of her reserve had disappeared.

Both children began the search with enthusiasm, shouting and exclaiming over each new find. Anslowe helped as well, his interest piqued. When they'd gathered a respectable collection, Emmeline looked around and picked up a stick of driftwood with a pointy end. She walked a little ways away and traced a circle with the stick. Then she rejoined them and drew a line in the sand. "Now, Tim, yours are the rocks and Emma, the shells are yours. You each get to throw five. Whoever throws the most in the circle, wins."

Anslowe smiled, watching the eager faces of the children.

Young Tim looked up at Emmeline with adoration. "Can I go first, please?" He spoke so correctly, save for the sweet lisp that thickened his words.

"Of course." She picked up a rock and handed it to him.

With a look of absolute concentration, the boy cocked back his arm and launched the rock. It landed far wide of the mark.

Emmeline commended him. "Well done, you have a good strong arm!"

Anslowe beamed, an unfamiliar sensation warming his chest. She had such a natural way with children, which made him all the more curious about her earlier reaction.

"Now it is Emma's turn." She beckoned the girl up to the line and handed her a shell.

Emma's throw was more hesitant and fell a little short of the circle. "So close," Emmeline praised. Then she picked up the stick and extended the line. "Now why don't you both try at the same time? Just be careful not to hit one another."

Emmeline handed them rocks and shells and they giggled and squealed with each new try. Both children had light hair and blue eyes, but he could envision a little girl with dark brown hair and eyes, a miniature version of Emmeline.

He stepped up to the line, wanting only to be closer to her. But if he stood there gawking he'd look like a lovesick fool. Instead, he knelt beside Tim in the sand, helping him with his aim. A moment later the boy launched his first rock right into the center of the circle. He cheered and embraced Anslowe, his tiny pudgy fingers squeezing Anslowe's neck.

"Tim, Emma. It is time to go back." Their nurse approached, her gray hair unruly in the breeze. "I hope they didn't bother you."

Anslowe stood and ruffled Tim's hair. "Not at all."

"They are dears." Emmeline smiled and bent down to face them. "You keep practicing," she instructed. "Perhaps we'll see you again."

The children waved goodbye and followed their nurse down the beach, turning to wave again every so often. Emmeline stood beside him, watching them go, the faint traces of a smile lining her cheeks. For a moment, with her so close, and with the children's echoes carried to them by the wind, it felt as if they were truly husband and wife.

He glanced down at the shells and rocks strewn in and around the circle Emmeline had drawn in the sand. Anslowe knew he had far to go, but with practice and effort, he too would improve, could become a worthy husband. Surely he could win the heart of the woman who stood at his side. His wife.

With a gentle smile tugging at his lips, he reached down and interlaced Emmeline's fingers with his own.

CHAPTER 11

*A*nslowe was disappointed not to have been seated within speaking distance of the prince regent at dinner. Not that he would have interrupted the man's favorite pastime—eating—with talk of political matters. But Prinny was known for singling out and bestowing attention on anyone who pleased or amused him. Sitting close to him would have made that a great deal easier.

After dinner, when the men were left to themselves, talk turned to the newly built Pavilion and its lavish furnishings. Every man seemed eager to ply Prinny as they heaped praise upon his new abode. Anslowe found himself more than annoyed with the scene and had little desire to become a part of the fray. Prinny fairly glowed under their praise, laughing and jesting, their noise swelling and reaching raucous levels.

Relief bloomed in his chest when Prinny stood and announced it was time to rejoin the ladies. The prince regent sniggered and turned to Uncle Garvey. "I do hope to sit right next to your wife. She brings me more amusement than anything."

If Anslowe were wise he would join them, waiting as the crowds thinned so that he might have a word before the prince regent left.

But his gaze landed on Captain Sharpe, and he quickly recalled his promise to Emmeline. She'd said the matter was urgent, and he didn't wish to disappoint her.

Twenty minutes later, the two of them sat together in the library, and Captain Sharpe had explained the situation regarding the men on trial for mutiny. Anslowe had asked a few pointed questions, mostly listening. In that brief time, he'd developed a great deal of respect for the captain, who was self-assured but not pompous, direct but not impertinent. He admired the captain's candor, even in the face of his own wrong-doing and wished to help him.

But the way in which he could help…it was yet to be seen whether Captain Sharpe would be amenable to such methods. The man sat with strict military posture, and his gray blue eyes seemed to see things only in black and white.

Anslowe sighed inwardly, keeping his face devoid of any show of emotion. "Captain Lloyd doesn't care for the common man, but he does care for his own skin. If he refuses to listen to what you shared with me, then it would be a shame if the Naval Appropriations Committee, or his wife in England, were to take legal action over his indiscretions." He notched his chin, thinking of the wives Captain Lloyd had taken in both Jamaica and India.

Captain Sharpe rose, letting out a cough. He moved to the fireplace. "Forgive me for saying so, my lord, but I have always viewed blackmail as the coward's way."

Anslowe got to his feet as well and folded his arms. "I agree with you, captain. And yet, in this instance the means could justify the end."

The captain, however, bristled at the suggestion that several members of the committee might need to be coerced. Captain Sharpe's gaze grew pointed. "In all seriousness, my lord, an overt threat could ruin my career." He shifted in his seat. "Captain Lloyd is known for ferocious feuds and villainizing his enemies."

Anslowe didn't flinch, even though he could sense the captain wrestling with himself and his sense of honor. But politics was an arena where Anslowe was master. He knew precisely when a cause was worth risking oneself, when the ends justified the means. And he knew what was at stake for the men accused of mutiny.

He didn't waste time mincing words. "If you have any integrity, then this is the right course. If you are not willing to risk your own career for the good of your men, then you don't have any business serving as captain."

Captain Sharpe squeezed his eyes shut and Anslowe knew he'd hit a nerve. He let his words settle for a moment. The captain ran his hands through his hair.

Anslowe spoke softly, with no condemnation. "I don't like seeing seamen abused unjustly, Captain Sharpe. Or suffering the harsh consequences for another's crimes."

"Neither do I." The man's response, his posture, told Anslowe he'd made up his mind. Politics could be a messy business. But it was these kinds of moments, where Anslowe knew he'd helped someone, that motivated him, and kept him pushing through.

The men talked for a few more minutes and when they'd finished, Captain Sharpe leaned forward. "My lord, I can't thank you enough." The two of them shook hands.

"It is my pleasure." It took some effort to bite back the grin that threatened. "Before you save the world, I hope you will take care of your own interests. I believe a certain lady would appreciate your company this evening. She did hold you in high enough regard to enlist my wife's assistance, after all." Speaking the words aloud only made Anslowe anxious to seek out Emmeline.

Captain Sharpe chuckled. "That is one area I do not need counsel to act."

* * *

EMMELINE SAT in conversation with Miss Marleigh and Lady Felicity. She did her best not to yawn, despite the way her jaw ached to open. A furtive glance at the clock on the mantle indicated the late hour, yet she'd not yet seen any sign of her husband. He'd very likely been pulled into a conversation and wouldn't notice the time until long after she'd retired to bed.

Which was probably for the best. She could hardly go ten seconds without remembering the sensation of Anslowe's lips upon hers, the concentrated attention, the look of desire in his eyes. For her. It was unfathomable, really. Even now in the crowded drawing room, hours later, the memory of his nearness stirred an answering desire within her.

At the approach of a footman, Emmeline glanced up in surprise. He came and stood next to her and she rose to her feet. He whispered quietly. "Excuse me, Lady Anslowe, but you have a visitor waiting in the front hall."

Emmeline pursed her lips, trying to imagine who might be visiting her here in Brighton, and at this hour. Perhaps the visitor was, in fact, for Lord Anslowe. She turned and followed the footman to the front hall. She didn't see anyone at first, until a figure stepped from behind the pillar that had been shielding her from view.

"Hello, Emmeline."

Emmeline gasped. It was Mama, her wrinkled attire attesting to long miles of travel. She hadn't seen her mother in almost a year and was not prepared for it. Her knees quaked, a host of unpleasant memories slithering through her stomach.

"Mama? What are you doing here?" It had only been two days previous that she'd written and informed Mama of her stay in Brighton. How could she possibly have received the letter and traveled here already?

"I should have known you'd be ungracious." Mama's eyes held a spiteful scrutiny.

"I'm sorry, Mama. I was only surprised to see you." The apology rolled off her tongue. How quickly she stepped into old habits. "When did you arrive in Brighton?" She hated the familiar wobble in her voice, but she was quite out of practice shielding herself from Mama's sharp words. Such a shield was never necessary with her husband.

"This afternoon," Mama said sharply. "And it is important I speak to you at once."

"Mama, I am sure the Garveys would be glad to have you join us in the drawing—"

Her words were cut off when Mama took ahold of her forearm, her grip so fierce Emmeline almost cried out in pain. "We are not here to *socialize*." She spat the word.

"Mrs. Drake, what an unexpected surprise." Emmeline turned her head, only to see her husband standing behind her, his voice calm and steady, yet his words clipped enough to carry a vague threat.

Mama released her hold on Emmeline, a forced expression of excitement replacing her angry mien. "Oh, it is the most delightful of surprises. Imagine you being here in Brighton. Such a fortunate coincidence."

Emmeline looked down at the welt on her arm, an angry red from Mama's bracing grip. Heaven help her, all she could think of was how her mother's arrival would affect things with Anslowe. Their marriage was like a tender new branch, incapable of withstanding strong winds. And Mama was a formidable gale that could end up snapping the branch clean off, long before it ever had a chance to grow thick and strong.

"Fortunate, indeed." Only from spending so much time in his company these past few days could Emmeline detect the falseness in his tone.

Anslowe's hand found a resting spot on her back, but his touch was tense. "I am sure we will see you another time, but we have had a long and busy day. Emmeline is exhausted and what kind of husband would I be if I didn't see that she gets the rest she needs?"

"Oh, but of course! And we will be very busy in Brighton. Our company is very much in demand." Her voice was overly sweet, cloying even.

"Good night, Mama. I do hope we see you again."

"Of course, of course!" Mama crowed.

Anslowe merely bowed, the movement stiff and formal. He extended his arm and led Emmeline out of the entry hall and up the stairs toward their room.

Emmeline hardly knew what to think. Anslowe seemed angry, but she wasn't certain—she'd never seen him angry before. Upset, yes. He'd been upset the other night when she'd confronted him. But tonight she sensed a silent fury, just beneath the surface, as if it might be wise to keep her distance.

When they reached their rooms, he pushed the door open and motioned for her to go ahead. She released his arm, and blew out a breath, trying to release the tension that had knotted inside her from the minute she'd laid eyes on Mama.

* * *

ANSLOWE WAS RARELY MOVED to anger. He'd been taught by his father to keep a tight rein on his emotions, that no one had power to make him feel anything he didn't wish to feel. And though he'd been upset several times as a young boy, he'd quickly discovered that anger was rarely productive.

But right now he was livid. His limbs bristled with indignation, and it was all he could do to hold himself in check. He'd not missed the way her mother had gripped her, as if Emmeline could be forced to do her bidding by mere physical coercion. He remained civil with the woman, but his self-control had been taxed to its limits.

Anslowe guided Emmeline over to the small sofa in their sitting room and sat down beside her. Her trembling hadn't abated and neither had his anger. But he could tell she feared his anger was directed at her.

She dropped his arm at once.

"I'm sorry. I did not know Mama was in Brighton. Were you interrupted from speaking with the prince regent? I know how much you wished to speak to him."

In truth, when Anslowe had seen Emmeline in her mother's clutches, he'd forgotten all about his pursuit of an audience with Prinny.

"No. In fact, I had just come from a meeting with Captain Sharpe."

She looked up, surprise flickering through her features. "Captain Sharpe?"

"Yes. I am glad you urged me to speak with him. The matter troubling him is worth pursuing."

She reached over and grasped his arm, squeezing gently. "Oh, thank you. Miss Brook will be so grateful."

In that moment, Anslowe could hardly bring himself to care that he'd missed a chance with Prinny. Not with Emmeline's gratitude shining in her eyes. It seemed so small a thing to have elicited such a response. "Your gratitude is enough for me."

A hint of a smile stole over her face.

Much as he hated to dim it, he needed to address the matter that had brought his temper dangerously close to the surface. "Emmeline, did your mother say why she is here?"

Her smile dropped. "No. Though she seemed upset about something."

A quick glance confirmed that the pale skin of Emmeline's arm was already bruising from her mother's harsh treatment. He took her arm, tracing the discolored area with his fingers.

"Has she always been that way?"

She ducked her head and gave a subtle nod. He contemplated that for a moment.

Her hands twisted in her lap. "What I said earlier…about not wanting children. It isn't true. I do want them." Emmeline breathed out. "But I'm afraid. Afraid of being like her." She winced.

He shook his head, the action almost involuntary. "Impossible. There isn't an ounce of unkindness in you. Of that I am sure." He lifted her chin, forcing her to meet his gaze. "When the time comes, you shall make an excellent mother."

He cleared his throat. "But, to the matter at hand. She has no right to speak to you that way. Or touch you." He tried to keep his voice gentle despite the fierce protectiveness that welled up inside him. "You are now my wife, and your protection is my right. I don't want you to be alone with her."

Emmeline's dark eyes sought his, searching, probing. Her eyes shimmered and she dropped her gaze suddenly, her lashes heavy with tears. "Thank you."

Not trusting himself to speak, Anslowe bowed his head over Emmeline's arm and pressed a kiss to her bruised and tender skin, vowing not to let anyone hurt her again.

CHAPTER 12

Sleep did not come easily to Emmeline. How could it when she could still feel the ghost of her husband's lips pressed against her skin? A token, a promise, to care for her. *Your protection is my right.*

Whatever defenses she had mounted to safeguard her heart had crumbled at his words, his touch. She loved him. So fiercely she ached with it.

From the time she was a young girl, Emmeline had been slapped and pinched, her bruises and marks physical evidence of Mama's displeasure. Over time the marks always faded and eventually disappeared. But Mama's words of belittlement, scorn, and disparagement never did. A constant stream of censure echoed in Emmeline's head, Mama's harsh voice never more than a thought away.

As she'd grown older, she'd learned to guard against the assaults, to distance herself from Mama's cruelty. She never flinched. She rarely cried. She remained aloof, the distance between her head and her heart its own form of armor.

After her marriage to Anslowe, the harsh voice in her head had faded over time. Yet in Mama's presence tonight, the reverberating effects had come back with startling swiftness.

Until, in one heartbeat, she'd seen something that threatened to be her undoing. A man, so gentle and good, so fierce in her defense, that he promised to fight her battles for her. Her chest radiated with a joy that was almost painful. Was it any wonder she couldn't sleep?

Perhaps a biscuit would do the trick. She sat up and reached for the candle. Her hand hit something, and with a crash loud enough to wake the entire household, the vase that had adorned her bedside table hit the blunt edge of the table and shattered.

The noise startled her nearly half to death. Emmeline didn't move, afraid she would cut herself on the glass that had gone flying in all directions, including all over the coverlet.

A quick knock sounded at the door and through the pale moonlight she could make out her husband's outline as he pushed the door open. "Emmeline! Are you all right?"

She nodded, then realized he probably couldn't see her. "Yes. I knocked the vase down and broke it." She cleared her throat. "There is glass everywhere."

"Do you have a candle?"

"I think it rolled under the bed."

He took several long strides toward the trunks in the corner of the room. "There are more in your trunks?"

She grew hesitant. "No. I gave them away."

"You gave them…away?"

She didn't need to see his face to hear the incredulity in his tone. "Yes. So many of the other guests needed them, and we brought so many extra…"

"Trust you to give away all our candles." A low chuckle. "I used the last of mine tonight. Let me fetch my boots."

He was gone only a moment, and then he was crunching across the scattered shards of glass toward her bedside. "You can't sleep in here tonight. We can send for someone to clean this up in the morning." With great care he pulled back the blankets and then placed an arm behind her shoulders and scooped her into his arms.

The darkness only heightened Emmeline's other senses. The sure stride of her husband, the strength in his arms that enfolded her so effortlessly. The scent of him—musky and masculine. He carried her through the sitting room and used his shoulder to push open the door to his own chamber. Her heart beat swiftened, seemed as though it might press through the thin material of her nightdress. He laid her gently on his bed and she missed his warmth, his nearness at once.

Silver moonlight arced through the window and brightened the coverlet. "I can sleep out on the sofa tonight," he said.

It had all happened so suddenly, Emmeline didn't know what to say. Didn't know what she wanted. But just the thought of being here, where he slept—

He stepped back and moved the vase which rested on his bedside table to the far side. A jesting smile. "Should I move it further away, or do you think you can manage not to break this one as well?"

"I'm not sure teasing should be allowed at this hour of the night," she said with feigned crossness, but he only laughed. She swung her legs over the side of the bed and got to her feet. "I can take the sofa. There's no need for you to give up your bed."

"Emmeline—"

"Truly." She placed a hand on his chest, then realized her mistake. His shirt was open at the neck, and her palm touched skin. His heart galloped as quickly as her own. "Anslowe," she breathed.

"Emmeline." His voice was thick, almost strangled.

Of its own volition, her hand traced upward, past his chest to his throat, up the column of his neck. He swallowed. Her thumb brushed his chin, his jaw, then his lips. He froze. His breath grew jagged.

Desire pulsing in her fingertips, she tilted his head down and urged him closer. With a soft breath his lips pressed to hers, and heat flowed straight to her center. His lips were warmth, light, and safety. Insistent but not demanding. Hopeful but patient. Bridled passion that gave her every opportunity to pull away.

It was Anslowe who finally stepped back. His eyes glassy, his breathing labored.

She stepped toward him.

He gently took her wrist. "I want to wait, Emmeline. Until you are ready. Until you are certain of me. Of us. I don't ever want you to believe that this—" he motioned between them, "is all I want." He glanced over at the door.

Disappointment and relief both trickled through her. Yet the thought of him walking away left her feeling empty. "Will you stay? And just hold me?"

He closed his eyes a moment and then nodded. He removed his boots.

She slipped into the mussed bed, hesitant and vulnerable and exposed. But all of that disappeared as the warmth of his chest pressed against her back. He picked up her braid and set it to rest over her shoulder. "That tickles."

She smiled in the dark as he settled his weight and his legs brushed hers. "Anslowe?"

"Hmmm?"

"Thank you. For protecting me from my mother." She gulped, tears pricking her eyes. The solid form of him against her was comforting. A shield.

He squeezed her shoulder and she could feel the tension in the lines of his body. She breathed in and out slowly, hoping to help him relax. And finally, finally, his rigidity lessened. His breaths lengthened. And sleep pulled them both into its firm embrace.

* * *

BLISSFUL AGONY. It was the only way to describe the way it felt to hold Emmeline in his arms, her dark lashes fanning against milky skin, her expression peaceful. Dawn had just begun, the moon's thumbnail still visible against the colorless sky.

Emmeline let out a sweet little breath and adjusted one leg. His lips hungered for another taste of her. The torture became too much and Anslowe eased himself back. Once he was certain he wouldn't wake her, he put his feet to the floor and pulled on his boots. He glanced back at her sleeping figure and imagined what it would be like to wake up with her by his side each morning. A fierce yearning, a wanting, swelled up inside of him.

They would get there, of that he was certain. But not yet. Something about the darkness and the moonlight had woven a spell around the two of them in this room. Exquisite moments he treasured, and not just her kisses. The sweet way she implored him to stay, and the trust it implied. The way her body sighed against his as he'd held her.

But if he stayed, he could well imagine there would be discomfort, some shyness and embarrassment when she awoke. The daylight might undo the progress they'd made. And he couldn't stand the thought of last night's magic being stripped away.

So he quietly gathered his things and left the room. He had a great deal to do and there wasn't a moment to waste.

CHAPTER 13

*E*mmeline allowed herself the luxury of a few extra moments in bed. She'd slept better last night than any of the other nights since their arrival in Brighton. She blinked her eyes open. The room was unfamiliar, and suddenly it all came racing back. The broken vase, Anslowe carrying her into his room, the kisses they'd shared. Oh heavens. She truly was lost to him.

But she was alone. A quick glance confirmed his boots were gone. Did he regret staying with her through the night? A thread of uncertainty needled its way through her euphoria at his absence. If only she could have woken in his arms.

She stretched her arms above her head and the pain in her arm brought back other, less pleasant memories. Namely, Mama's unexpected appearance last night. She didn't move from the bed. When she got up, she would have to think of the possibility of dealing with Mama again, but under the covers, Emmeline could push such thoughts away, and revel in thoughts of her husband. Anslowe's hand at her back as he led her away from Mama. The gentle slope of his cheeks that were so often raised in a smile. The golden warmth of his brown eyes, like dark wood lit up by the rays of the sun.

Her fingers toyed with the end of her braid, unable to shake away the grin that lifted her cheeks.

A knock sounded at the door, and Bridget walked in. "Lord Anslowe requests your company in the sitting room for breakfast as soon as possible. But I suppose you'll need me to go and fetch your things." A mischievous grin lit Bridget's face.

Emmeline sat straight up. Her cheeks flamed red at Bridget's teasing. "Yes," she said, with a decorum that belied her inward giddiness. "Please bring me my things."

Bridget smirked.

"What are you not telling me?" demanded Emmeline, her suspicions aroused.

Bridget sighed, going dreamy eyed. "His attentions toward you, my lady. I've never seen their like." And she refused to say anymore and hurried to go fetch Emmeline a dress and some hair pins.

She returned with a white dress embroidered with a subtle diamond pattern. "This one?"

Emmeline nodded. She tried not to show her anxiousness as Bridget helped her dress and arranged her hair, but the whole process took an eternity.

When she finally slipped out of her door, Anslowe got to his feet. Seeing him again, each time, she was startled by his stark handsome features, which were softened by his tender smile. Why must she feel so terribly awkward again? Her mouth grew dry.

He crossed to meet her and enveloped her hands in his own. "I wish you joy of your birthday, Emmeline."

Her mouth dropped open. Her birthday! Was it Saturday already?

He smiled knowingly. "Did you forget your own birthday?"

She bit her lip. "I suppose I did. At home I am always closely aware which day it is, but I suppose I've lost track of the calendar. How did you know?"

"A husband must know his wife's birthday and be sure to make it memorable."

Emmeline glanced down at the breakfast tray, overflowing with delicacies for the second day in a row. "At this rate, my lord, I shan't be able to fit into the carriage when we return home."

"Then I shall be forced to limit you to two pastries." He winked at her. "And you might need to eat faster than is ladylike. We are off to see the Pavilion. Our tour begins at ten."

"The Pavilion? I didn't know they did tours."

"Not everyone is given a tour. Only women with birthdays and especially convincing husbands."

"I suppose I should consider myself fortunate." Though she made light of it, her heart felt as though it might burst with joy.

"Most fortunate," he said, his tone full of teasing. "Now, not a moment to waste."

The Pavilion was more splendid than Emmeline could have imagined. The gardens were a sight in and of themselves, the emerald greenery enveloping the structure, contrasting against the tannish gold walls. Emmeline had seen pictures of the Taj Mahal, and the similarities between the two were not lost on her. The intricate lattice work, the numerous spires almost took her breath away. Inside, the colors were flamboyant, the furnishings luxurious.

The man giving them a tour, one of the aides of the regent, boasted about the delicacy of the construction and the astronomical costs.

She thanked their guide when the tour ended and then laid a hand on Anslowe's arm. "Thank you. It was as magnificent as I'd hoped."

"A little too grand for my taste, but I'd say it fits Prinny. The colors, the design. The décor rather looks like his outlandish outfits."

"It does seem fitting."

He pulled something from his pocket. It was a small package, wrapped in paper and tied with twine. "It isn't much, but I thought a gift was in order."

"There's no need. This tour was gift enough."

"A man should have the right to spoil his wife a little, if he chooses."

"I suppose," she agreed.

"You suppose? Where is the fun in being married if I can't spoil you?"

"Surely there are other things that would be considered more fun than—" She blushed at her unwitting implication.

He gave her a knowing grin. "Ah well, there are most definitely other things to look forward to. But for now, spoiling you will suffice. Here."

He handed her the package and led her to an out-of-the-way bench behind a large topiary. "Now open it."

Emmeline untied the twine and pulled back the paper, revealing a perfect miniature of the Pavilion, about the size of her fist. She lifted a hand to her mouth in wonder.

"I thought we could start a collection of mementos, of souvenirs. A little something to remember our first trip together. The first of many, since we are to go overseas this fall. We can get one in Paris, in Venice . . ."

It was so considerate, so lovely. For now she would not only remember this trip, but the thoughtfulness of the man who had brought her. "I don't know what to say."

"You like it then?" Such hopefulness lifted his voice.

"It is perfect. The loveliest gift I have ever received." With Anslowe beside her, she felt completely content. She ran her thumb along the ridges in the roofline and joy nestled into her heart.

* * *

THEY BROWSED up and down the streets, and Anslowe spoiled her far more than he should have. He treated her to ices at a little local shop in The Lanes. They stopped and bought more candles, laughing quietly about the absurdity of his aunt. With a knowing smile, he made her promise not to give them away. In a quaint little book store he insisted on purchasing her a book on the sights of Paris so she could determine what she most wanted to see. He bought some pearl-studded pins for her hair, though she insisted she didn't need them.

"Am I only allowed to buy you what you need?" he asked. "That's quite a notion."

"You have worn me out with your spoiling. Shouldn't we be getting back?"

"I suppose you are right," he agreed.

As their carriage approached Havencrest, they saw a group of guests gathered on the lawn. Gigs of all shapes and sizes were preparing for a race and the crowd's noise levels rose as word spread of the prince regent's arrival.

Emmeline didn't miss the way Anslowe looked toward the royal carriage. "You need to speak with him. Go ahead."

Before he could protest, she added, "I insist," with a firm voice.

"Very well. But be it known, I am going against my will." He tipped his hat at her.

"Of course." She looked heavenward. "Who wouldn't prefer my company to the prince regent's?"

"Ridiculous woman, you underestimate yourself." She loved the teasing quality of his voice, the way he found a way to compliment her even when she didn't deserve it.

"Good sir, please tell me one quality I possess that would make me better company than Prince George."

The carriage stopped and Anslowe stepped out, still smiling. "How am I to choose?" he asked in a flirtatious tone. "You have many enticing qualities, Lady Anslowe." He leaned over her hand and kissed it before releasing her fingers.

Something shifted in that moment, a pinch in Emmeline's chest, though she couldn't quite put a name to her unease. The words sounded so...familiar. A bolt of recognition shot through her, for those were the exact words he'd said to Miss Hastings a year ago. *You have many enticing qualities, Miss Hastings.*

"Emmeline, are you all right?"

Her stomach swooped, almost as if she were falling. The icy sweet she'd shared with her husband turned to acid in her stomach, burning a path back up her throat. "I'm just tired is all," she managed. "I'll return to the house for some rest."

Suddenly she was questioning everything her husband said to her.

Did he even care for her, as he'd made her believe? Or was this all some elaborate ploy to ensure the safety of his political maneuverings? Unshed tears burned her eyes, the scenery outside passing by in a blur.

Back at the house she hurried through the front door. For once the cavernous entry way seemed quiet, as all of the guests, or at least most of them, were outside. Thank goodness. She needed to collect her thoughts, to try and somehow shore up the cracking sensation in her heart.

She breathed in through her mouth and exhaled, grasping at logic. It could easily have been a coincidence. The memory of that exact phrase, spoken to another, was jarring to say the least. But she'd give Anslowe the benefit of the doubt and speak to him about it. Surely what she'd felt between them hadn't all been imagined. The nausea abated once she decided upon that course of action.

But when she walked into their shared sitting room, her parents sat on the sofa, waiting for her. She halted her steps, shock jerking her from her previous thoughts.

"There you are. We've been waiting for you for over an hour." Mama tapped a fan against her knee.

Apprehension clutched at Emmeline. Something was wrong. Normally in a place like Brighton, Mama would be out and about, seeing and being seen.

"We are in dire need, Emmeline. Of money. Of your husband's protection."

Emmeline pinched her lips together. "Whatever do you mean?"

"The speculation. We lost everything. And many men, many powerful men, are pointing fingers, blaming your father."

Though Emmeline wasn't well acquainted with her father's finances, she'd always known his propensity for taking risks. Her insides trembled. "Was it his fault?"

Her mother scoffed. "Of course not, how can you ask such a thing? Speculation is risky by nature."

But why would her father undertake such risks when they'd had so much? It didn't make sense! "Who knows?" she demanded.

"Everyone in London. We came here, hoping to escape the rumors."

"Mama, Brighton is less than a day's travel from London! All of the *ton* is summering here."

"We went to Chelten House first, only to be informed you were here," Papa said, his voice even. Ever the level-headed businessman. His head hung low, and Emmeline had never seen him so discouraged. His sharp eyes, usually keen on a business deal looked dull. His skin sagged, as if he'd aged ten years since she'd last seen him.

Emmeline's head was spinning, trying to take it all in. "What is it you think I can—"

Mama got to her feet. "Do not act as if you are above us! We gave you everything—why without your dowry you would be nothing!"

The strange thing was, now that she'd known Anslowe's tender love and care, it was easy to see how very little her parents loved her. The knowledge strengthened her, and she determined not to be guilted into succumbing to Mama's demands.

First, it was imperative she gather information. "Tell me, Mama. Who else lost money in the scheme?"

"You know Mr. Tillington and Sir Reginald. Many men risked smaller amounts. But it is Lord Sotheby who your father fears will see him ruined."

Lord Sotheby. No—No! Worry clenched Emmeline's gut and a pulsing rush of blood against her temples signaled the beginnings of a headache. Anslowe. What would this do to him? Why, of anyone, did it have to be the man Anslowe was counting on for support of his bill? Her hands began to tremble. "How bad is it?"

"We lost everything," her father replied.

"The house?" she asked in disbelief.

"Gone."

"You must help us, Emmeline," her mother screeched. "We need money, the chance to make a fresh start."

Emmeline shut her eyes, willing herself to remain calm. There was little to stir empathy toward her mother, but her father looked so forlorn, so disheartened. He'd never been intentionally cruel with her, perhaps only too preoccupied to see how desperately his daughter needed a loving parent.

"It is only recently that Lord Anslowe's estates have begun to turn a profit. We do not have a great deal of extra income." But the money was the least of her concerns. Something of this magnitude could have the power to destroy Anslowe's political career. She could imagine her husband's disappointment, his frustration when he learned the truth.

He would regret marrying her. He'd wish he'd proposed to Miss Hastings, whose family would never subject him to such public disgrace. He'd despise Emmeline once her connections ruined his political aspirations.

"I will do what I can to help you, but I need time," she finally choked out. And she had to determine how best to shield Anslowe from this catastrophe. "Tell me where you are staying and I will contact you once I have sorted things out."

Emmeline was so full of anguish she scarcely took note of her parents' goodbyes. Her mind swirled and tangled, desperate to lay hold on something—anything—that might help thwart disaster. Surely there had to be something she could do to protect her husband.

When Anslowe came to escort her down to dinner, she claimed a headache. She knew she was pale, almost feverish with worry, so she wasn't lying when she said she didn't feel well enough to be among company.

"I don't like to leave you looking so unwell," he worried.

His words only deepened her anguish and filled her with guilt. She couldn't meet his eyes.

The truth itched to be told, but Emmeline couldn't bear to think on how the tenderness in his expression would be replaced with loathing. He would see her as a liability, someone who had taken away everything he'd worked for.

"There's something you aren't telling me. Earlier, in the carriage, something upset you." He reached out and clasped her hand in his. "What is it, Emmeline?"

"I—" Tears balanced upon her lashes. For some reason she couldn't explain, she went on. "It was silly, really. Something you once said to Miss Hastings. You said the exact same thing to me this afternoon."

"What was it?" His mouth ticked down.

The words struggled for release. "You have many enticing qualities, Miss Hastings."

"Oh, Emmeline." He considered her words for a moment, not rushing to a hasty response. The solemn look in his eyes promised her concern mattered to him. "Words are often spoken too casually, and I myself am guilty of such offense. But I would use an example, if I may." He looked to her for approval.

She gave a quick nod.

"Do you know how in a ballroom, you greet dozens of people, saying hello over and over again. But then, when you see a dear friend, and use the same word as a greeting for them, it means much more, because of how you feel toward them?"

Her mouth grew dry and she bobbed her head.

"You can rest assured that there was no meaning behind what I once said to Miss Hastings. As you well know, I'd forgotten I almost offered for her." He squeezed her hand. "But I meant what I said this afternoon. You *do* have many enticing qualities. Indeed Emmeline, you have quite enchanted me." Sincerity edged the tone of his voice, and it was impossible to disbelieve him.

But oh, believing him only made it that much worse. He was coming to care for her, perhaps even love her, and how could she bear it when all that was stripped away from her when he found out the truth?

"Yes, yes I understand. Forgive me for doubting you." Shame weighed heavily upon her, thickened her throat. "Please make my apologies to everyone downstairs. I just need to rest."

With a gentle kiss pressed to her hairline, he left her.

Bridget brought up a resplendent tray—soups and jellies, roasted vegetables, fish, and three kinds of meat. But Emmeline couldn't eat a single bite.

Not long after the dinner hour, a knock at the door surprised

Emmeline. Surely Anslowe was still in company with the gentlemen. But it was Mrs. Garvey who appeared in the doorway.

She looked at the untouched tray. "An unforgivable waste."

"I'm sorry. I don't feel well enough to eat."

"It's not your fault. It's my appalling husband. He has not an ounce of sense in his entire being."

Emmeline couldn't think of a polite response to that, so she stayed quiet.

Mrs. Garvey approached the bed. "You are ill?" Without asking permission she put her hand on Emmeline's forehead. "You don't have a fever. What ails you?"

This woman might be the very last woman on earth Emmeline had ever imagined confiding in. But her severe look coupled with Emmeline's frayed nerves, splintered all sense of propriety. Emmeline squeezed her eyes closed and tears spilled down her cheeks.

Mrs. Garvey pulled a chair from the corner of the room and gave a harrumphing sigh as she took a seat near the bed. "You aren't the kind to cry over a ripped dress or a ruined bonnet. So you must be crying over my nephew." Her brows pinched together. "Am I right?"

She could only nod.

The woman closed her eyes, as if it took every ounce of forbearance for her not to scoff. When she opened them, she leaned forward and took Emmeline's hand, patting it with her own. Emmeline was so startled by the tender gesture, her tears halted.

"You're young and you haven't been married long. While I won't claim to know everything, there are few people who wouldn't stand to benefit from my advice." She leaned forward. "Any tears shed for a man are wasted, that's what I say. All men suffer from a degree of stupidity. They can't help it. Once you learn that hard truth, you'll be far less prone to weeping."

If only the matter were that simple. Whatever Mrs. Garvey's opinion about men, Emmeline loved Anslowe, and her tears were evidence of that. Why else would she be crying if it wasn't because she feared losing him?

She blinked, forcing away the last of her tears. "I'll try to keep that in mind."

"See that you do. Now, I'll have one of the maids send up a cool cloth for your forehead. And no more crying." She rose to her feet and moved toward the door.

"Thank you, Aunt Garvey," Emmeline said softly.

The woman bowed her head. "Don't burn a candle tonight. You need to rest." And with that, she was gone, leaving Emmeline to suffer alone.

CHAPTER 14

*A*nslowe got away as quickly as he could, hoping for a word with Emmeline before she fell asleep. Their rooms were quiet, and Anslowe forewent knocking for fear of disturbing her. The gray wash of dusk allowed him light enough to see. Emmeline's eyes were closed, her dark brown hair splayed against the pillow, as if she hadn't taken the time to braid it, as was her habit. Her breaths were shallow, her cheeks still pale. But even in her unwell state, he thought her lovely. So innocent. So completely without guile.

He neared the bed, tempted by thoughts of laying beside her and taking her in his arms as he had the night before. Her eyelids were a pale purple color, almost bruised looking in the dim light. She shuddered a little, her hands clenching the coverlet before she relaxed.

Taking care to not make any noise, Anslowe knelt beside her. Her soft scent lingered near her pillow, lavender and honey. He watched the gentle rise and fall of her breath, wishing he could know what occupied her dreams. Was she beginning to care for him? Could she?

He brushed back a silken strand of hair from her head. She let out a deep breath at his touch and turned, her face toward his. Her lashes fluttered for a moment, but she didn't wake. With a quiet reverence he brushed a kiss to her temple. Before he was tempted to do more, he got to his feet.

He watched her a moment longer, and each moment he stayed, his chest swelled with feeling. Longing. He loved Emmeline. His love for her would deepen over time, yet he knew, all the same, that it was already there. Rooted within him, anxious to spread and grow. He took a moment, hallowed by it. It made him want to be better. More. A man who deserved such love in return.

* * *

SUNDAY WENT BY IN A BLUR. Guilt churned in Emmeline's stomach, as thick as the muddy water of the Thames. Though she didn't keep to her rooms, she barely managed to go through the motions. After Sunday services she sought out Miss Brook, who looked almost as forlorn as Emmeline felt. They walked the gardens in quiet companionship, content to be in one another's company without the need for burdensome conversation.

She avoided Anslowe, afraid he might learn the truth if he paid her too much attention. He came up behind her as she sat at her vanity, preparing to go down to dinner.

"Have I done something to offend you?"

Not wanting to arouse his suspicions, she met his gaze, but focused on the length of his eyelashes, so as not to be distracted by the earnestness that threatened to undo her. "Of course not."

"Something I said, then? I am a politician—I have a great deal of practice in offending people." He laughed a little, as if hoping to soften her towards him.

"No, my lord."

He frowned. Then he held up a finger. "I forgot to give you your last birthday present."

"Anslowe, there's no need—"

He pulled out a sleek black box from his jacket and opened it. Inside lay an elegant pearl necklace. The pearls shone in the candlelight, as perfect as fresh fallen snow. They were too much. She turned away and bowed her head, unable to bear it another moment.

"Emmeline, what is it?"

She looked up and met his eyes in the mirror. "I-I kept something from you." She could barely get the words out, even now that she'd decided to tell him. "It was selfish of me, I know. To want a little more time with you. Before you no longer look at me the way you are now." The tears welling in her eyes forced her to take a breath.

He set the box down, snapping the lid closed, then came and knelt at her side. "What do you mean, Emmeline? I cannot imagine—"

"Please, this is difficult enough. Let me say my piece before you make any promises or say things you'll come to regret."

His eyes grew troubled.

"You know how Mama came on Friday night?"

He nodded once, tersely. The whole of his attention was fixed on her.

"They—Mama and Papa—both came to see me yesterday. I am not sure if you are aware, but my father has been involved in a great deal of speculation. His ventures have always been risky. His risks have always paid off. But in this particular venture he involved some powerful men." She swallowed. "He lost everything. And so did they."

It was quiet for a heartbeat before Anslowe spoke. "Who?"

"Lord Sotheby."

Anslowe's jaw tightened. He got to his feet in one swift move, hands tense at his sides. "You learned of this yesterday?" His cheeks flushed with anger. "Why did you not tell me? In a situation such as this, every minute—every hour is vital."

"I am sorry," she whispered.

"I won't be at dinner," he said. "I must see if anything can be salvaged." He strode from the room and shut the door with a bang.

And tears, whether wasted or not, poured down Emmeline's cheeks.

* * *

ANSLOWE WAS IN A DARK MOOD. He sat in one of Brighton's local taverns, cursing the world as he drank. He'd called on Lord Sotheby this afternoon only to find the man even more bitter and unreasonable than he'd expected. Sotheby had refused to listen to a word he said and assured him he would never support any bill Anslowe presented in the House of Lords.

He traced the small rim of the glass with his finger. The whiskey fueled his sense of betrayal. All that he'd worked for, all of the connections he'd built. Votes called in, trades made. All for naught.

And what was worse, Emmeline had blindsided him, had kept the truth from him. Even now, anger flared within him as he remembered her confession. After they'd promised there would be no more secrets between them.

If he was honest with himself, he could acknowledge the fault wasn't hers. Yet his mind played over that night when she'd approached him a year ago. Miss Hastings had been on his arm. She was from an established family. Yet he'd laughed off Emmeline's concern of her father being in trade. Perhaps he shouldn't have.

The very thought filled him with guilt, and yet there it was. If he could have foreseen this, would he have made a different choice? He twisted his glass, watching the liquid swirl. He didn't know. Not that it mattered. What was done, was done.

He lifted the glass, poured the fiery liquid down his throat, and called for another.

CHAPTER 15

When Emmeline sat down with her parents, she felt none of the anxiety she was accustomed to in their presence. Instead, she felt powerful. She'd never had an easy time standing up for herself, but she was more than willing to stand up for Anslowe.

"Mama. Papa." She gave them each a curt nod. "I cannot offer you much, but I did the best I could." She held up an envelope containing the money she had earned by selling some of her jewelry at a small pawn shop in Brighton. "You said you wanted the chance for a fresh start, and that is what I am offering."

Her mother's eyes narrowed. Her father held his hands in his lap. Both remained silent.

"I have here close to five hundred pounds. It is not enough for you to live the lifestyle you are used to, but it is enough for you to begin again. Here is the condition on which it is offered. Your actions, whether intentional or not, have damaged my husband's political standing." She let out a breath, holding her head steady. "For you to stay here in England would only prolong the scandal and its effects. This money is given with the understanding that you start again else-where. America. Australia. India. Take your pick."

Mama let out a gasp. "Are you truly relegating us—your parents—to one of those heathenistic countries?"

"No. I am not. I am giving you a chance for a new beginning, with plenty of money to help you undertake new business ventures. It is up to you whether or not you deem the opportunity a worthy one."

Her mother sputtered, her face growing red. "Why you ungrateful—"

Her father nodded. "I have always wanted to see America. It is said to be a place where a man can make something of himself. And trade is not looked down upon."

"America? Why there isn't an ounce of sophistication in that cast-off country! Nothing but unrefined ruffians!"

"We are going, Sophia." Her father's tone was firm. "Thank you, Emmeline. You have been more than generous." He stood and reached out to her, patting her on the shoulder awkwardly.

"Generous?" her mother protested.

Emmeline handed him the envelope. "Please write. I wish the very best for you." She turned to her mother. "Goodbye, Mama." And with a sigh that yielded pent-up relief, she turned and left them to their argument.

A few hours later Emmeline eyed herself critically in the mirror. By all accounts she was ready for tonight's ball. Her deep red gown perfectly fitted. Her hair arranged to perfection by Bridget. Only the hollowness in her eyes hinted at the devastation within. Emmeline hadn't seen Anslowe since Sunday night before dinner. Two full days with no sign of him.

It was probably for the best. It meant he wasn't around to take notice of how Bridget had already packed her trunks. Emmeline's early departure had to be handled carefully. She would make a brief appearance at tonight's ball, slip away early, and then take a hired coach back to Chelten House. No one would notice her absence tomorrow morning in the hustle and bustle of all the guests departing.

It was time to go down where a waiting carriage would take her to the Royal Pavilion, yet she found small ways to put it off. Another glance in the mirror. A quick sweep of the room to make sure she wasn't forgetting anything. Her eyes caught on the miniature Pavilion Anslowe had given her, sitting atop her vanity. She picked it up and took it to the unlatched trunk, nestling it within some of the soft folds of her gowns. A sweet memory, however fleeting, of what might have been.

Once satisfied, she took the slim black box containing the pearl necklace Anslowe had given her. She crossed to his room, and left it, along with a note, atop his bureau. She pulled on her gloves, carefully covering the fading bruise Mama had left. The irony was not lost on her. She'd feared Mama for so long. Yet now she'd lost Anslowe's love. And the bruising of her heart hurt far worse than any pain Mama had ever inflicted.

* * *

ANSLOWE STARED OUT THE WINDOW. Trade ships sailed in and out of the harbor, yet he hardly saw them. He rolled his shoulders, trying to ease the ache along his spine. The inn where he'd stayed for the past two nights was hardly reputable, and the comfort of the bed left much to be desired. Yet he'd needed time to collect his thoughts, to sort out his feelings before he faced Emmeline.

He scuffed his boot against the floorboard. Lord Sotheby's own foolish investment was the cause of all this, but the man's need for a scapegoat would see all of Anslowe's aspirations ruined.

Years of work brought to nothing.

And yet the void in Anslowe's chest had little to do with his tattered political career.

A knock sounded at the door. Anslowe turned. "Come in."

A spindly looking man with graying hair grown over his ears stepped toward him. "My lord, the paper you've been waiting for has just arrived." He pressed it into Anslowe's hands.

"Thank you." Anslowe gave a curt nod and tipped the man.

He opened the paper, anxious for news of how the trial had gone. He scanned the article outlining the outcome and blew out a relieved breath. Captain Sharpe had followed through. Anslowe could at least take comfort knowing he'd done one last thing of value before his political influence was lost. Emmeline would be glad to hear about it as well, given her role in the matter.

But, no. Perhaps she wouldn't wish to speak to him at all. The very advice he'd given Captain Sharpe sprang to his mind. *If you are not willing to risk your own career for the good of your men, then you don't have any business serving as captain.* The chastisement mocked him. His own words, a knife to his gut.

Through the haziness in his brain, one thing became clear. He needed Emmeline. Loved her. And what must she think of him? That he cared more for his career than for her? How quickly he'd lost sight of what was important. There were plenty of men who could continue to fight for bills and squabble over votes. But only he had a duty to Emmeline. Stronger than any duty to the House of Lords.

Emmeline had been guilty of nothing more than being the bearer of bad news. Yet he'd blamed her and bolted at the first sign of trouble. The look in her eyes. It had nearly killed her to tell him the truth. Because she'd feared losing him. And she was right to fear, for how badly he'd reacted.

He needed to make things right with her. He called for a carriage, his patience thinning with every moment he had to wait. His mind urged the conveyance up the hill toward Havencrest.

The carriage slowed, and Anslowe peered out the window, trying to glimpse what had caused the driver to curb his speed. A long line of carriages waited to turn out the drive leading to the road that led down toward Brighton. The ball. He'd completely forgotten.

He tapped on the roof of the carriage. When the driver stopped, Anslowe swung the door open. "I'll walk from here." He cut across the wide meadow, hoping to avoid the bulk of the guests. He went around through the back doors.

Anslowe ran up the stairs, hoping he could catch Emmeline before she departed for the ball. Heaven knew he wasn't dressed for it with his unshaven face, his rumpled clothing. Emmeline's room was empty. Blast! He rang for his valet, nearly sending the man into a bout of fits with how much he hurried him.

He checked his cuffs one more time and then took one final glance in the mirror. And that was when he caught sight of the small black box resting atop the bureau, the very one containing the pearl necklace he'd given Emmeline for her birthday. Wedged inside was a note. He unfolded it and read quickly.

LORD ANSLOWE,

You cannot know how much I regret approaching you at the Ramsbury's ball a year ago. I acted selfishly, looking, hoping for an escape. What I never expected to find was a man who captured my heart. It is yours, Anslowe.

Your connection to me and my family has hurt you and for that I am deeply sorry. I will do everything within my power to shield you from the effects of my father's folly. I will make a brief appearance at the ball so as not to arouse any rumors, and then return to Chelten House tonight. Once there, I will pack my things and return to London where I will do my best to mount a case for an annulment.

No doubt this will cause some scandal, but I imagine with your title and standing it will die down quickly. Unfortunately, I cannot protect you from all the consequences my connections have brought, but hopefully your political allies will not hold your short-lived marriage to me against you.

Emmeline

ANSLOWE FELT as though the wind had been knocked out of him. Emmeline, gone? An annulment. The idea was preposterous for a thousand reasons, most importantly because he loved her! Hang his political allies!

He tucked the black case in his pocket and hurried from the room. He strode down the stairs and called for his carriage, ignoring greetings from several other guests. Never had such a short journey taken so long. The sight of the Pavilion, and the time spent there with Emmeline, made his chest ache with longing. She had to still be there. She had to be.

The ballroom was enormous by any standard, but doubly so when one was looking for a rather petite woman. He didn't even know what she was wearing. He glanced through the crowd continuously, his anxiousness growing as the hands on the clock nudged forward. He'd become nearly frantic when he finally caught sight of a dark-haired woman in a scarlet dress.

He was across the room in seconds, following her out onto the verandah. "Emmeline!"

She turned, her eyes going wide at the sight of him.

Words seemed too fragile, too tenuous to use in such a moment. Instead, he closed the distance between them and took her into his arms. She resisted only a moment before melting against him, her entire body trembling.

"I'm so very sorry," she cried.

The feel of her in his arms was heaven and he gathered her tightly to him. "The only thing you should feel sorry for is the note you left me." He pulled back, making sure she faced him squarely. "We had a bargain, remember?" He was trying to make light of the matter, yet suddenly his heart was so heavy, overflowing with love for the woman before him, he could hardly get the words out. "A *marriage* bargain. I don't want an annulment. My political career is nothing to me, without you."

She looked up at him with wide eyes, uncertainty still marking her expression.

He gazed at her fiercely, doing his best to convince her of his sincerity. "I am sorry if my poor reaction caused you to doubt me. I love you. And I want nothing more than to be worthy of a woman like you."

Tears streaked her face. "What of your political career?"

He took her face in his hands, brushing at her tears with his thumbs. "Lord Sotheby is bitter, but his wrath will pass. Everyone will know it was his own foolish ventures that brought his ruin. In a year or two, this will have been forgotten. And for now, we are free to travel—for as long as we'd like."

She half laughed, half sobbed. "Is that the silver lining then?"

"Only if there is a chance you haven't given up on me completely."

Emmeline shook her head. "How could I give up on the man who has captured my heart?" She smiled through her tears.

"Have I really?"

She nodded. "You have."

He drew her closer, staring at her with adoration. "I am well aware of how precious your heart is, Emmeline. And I promise to care for it, to guard it carefully."

"Oh, Anslowe. How I love you."

The words reverberated through him, resounding with the power of a lightning strike. Suddenly, the distance between them felt far too great. Anslowe leaned closer, and with the utmost gentleness, he kissed each of her cheeks, feeling the wetness of her tears. "And I, you." Then he brought his mouth to hers, his lips both insistent and tender. With her mouth beneath his, no words were necessary.

A seal, a promise.

The end of their bargain.

And the beginning of their marriage.

REGENCY HOUSE PARTY: HAVENCREST

If you enjoyed this story, please leave a review on Goodreads, Amazon, or Bookbub!
And be sure to check out the other titles in the Regency House Party: Havencrest Series

Miss Marleigh's Pirate Lord
The Vexatious Widow
Charmed by His Lordship
The Captain's Lady

ABOUT THE AUTHOR

At a young age Heidi perfected the art of hiding out so she could read instead of doing chores. One husband and four children later, not much has changed. She has an abiding love for peanut butter M&Ms, all things fall, and any book that can make her forget she is supposed to be keeping her children alive.

Heidi currently lives just north of Boston, in a charming old town in southern New Hampshire.

Connect with Heidi on her website: https://www.
authorheidikimball.com

Made in United States
Troutdale, OR
02/01/2024